DAVID MEANS

The Secret Goldfish

HARPER PERENNIAL

London, New York, Toronto and Sydney

Harper Perennial
An imprint of HarperCollins*Publishers*
77–85 Fulham Palace Road
Hammersmith
London W6 8JB

www.harperperennial.co.uk

This edition published by Harper Perennial 2006

1

First published in Great Britain by Fourth Estate 2005

ISBN-13 978-0-00-716488-2
ISBN-10 0-00-716488-2

Some of the stories in this book appeared in the following publications:
'The Secret Goldfish' in the *New Yorker*; 'Lightning Man' in *Esquire*;
'It Counts as Seeing' in *Harper's*; 'Sault Ste. Marie' in *Harper's*; 'Blown from the
Bridge' and 'A Visit from Jesus' (as 'Two Folktales from Michigan') in *Witness*;
'Elyria Man' in *McSweeney's*; 'The Project' in the *Alaska Quarterly Review* and
Harper's; 'Carnie' in *Witness* and *The Best American Mystery Stories, 2001*

Typeset in Belén

Printed and bound in Great Britain by Clays Ltd, St Ives plc

The unsaid is written, eloquently
...chieve the impact of chill-
...troversy', *Irish Times*

...rangely

From the reviews of *The*

'There's something exquisite
Means's unflinching vision . . . The
medium; in his hands, it seems as ele.
landscape from which he patiently carves it
places you don't want to visit, but makes you u
you have to go there'   *Daily*

'Means is a fine writer, superior to many of his more famo
contemporaries . . . His prose is often masterful. The way he
handles small, incidental observations is particularly relish-
able . . . He knows exactly how to conjure up vivid realities
with a minimum of words'   MICHEL FABER, *Guardian*

'Run out and buy a copy now . . . Means is menacingly funny,
profound, relentless, unnervingly original and capable of seeing life, particularly its tiny, unforgiving details, with a clarity

By the same author

A Quick Kiss of Redemption
Assorted Fire Events

To Genève

[CONTENTS]

Lightning Man   1

Sault Ste. Marie   15

It Counts as Seeing   33

Blown from the Bridge   47

A Visit from Jesus   61

Petrouchka [with Omissions]   69

Elyria Man   89

The Project   107

Hunger   113

Counterparts   131

Dustman Appearances to Date   147

Carnie   157

The Nest   171

Michigan Death Trip   187

The Secret Goldfish   197

THE
SECRET
GOLDFISH

The pure products of America
go crazy—

WILLIAM CARLOS WILLIAMS

[LIGHTNING MAN]

The first time, he was fishing with Danny. Fishing was a sacrament, and therefore, after the strike, when his head was clear, there was the blurry aftertaste of ritual: the casting of the spoon in lazy repetitions, the slow cranking, the utterance of the clicking reel, the baiting of the clean hook, and the cosmic intuitive troll for the deep pools of cool water beneath the gloss of a wind-dead afternoon. Each fish seemed to arrive as a miracle out of the silence: a largemouth bass gasping for air, gulping the sky, gyrating, twisting, turning against the leader's force. But then he was struck by lightning and afterward felt like a fish on the end of the line. There was a paradigm shift: he identified purely—at least for a few months—with the fish, dangling, held by an invisible line tossed down from the heavens.

∴

Lucy had languid arms and pearly-white skin—as smooth as the inside of a seashell, he liked to say—and he smelled, upon returning to the house on the Morrison farm one night, her peaty moistness on his fingers. He'd touched her—just swept his fingers into wetness—and now, unable to sleep, he'd gone outside to the porch swing to let the adrenaline subside. His hope was to score with her before he left for boot camp. A storm was coming. Sheets of heat lightning unfurled inside clouds to the west. Deep, laryngeal mumbles of thunder smothered the cricket noise. The bolt that hit him ricocheted off a fence twenty yards away. Later he would recall that he'd half-jokingly spoken to the storm, and even to God, in a surge of testosterone-driven delight. Come on, you bastards, give me what you've got—the same phraseology boys his age would soon be using to address incoming mortar rounds on East Asian battlefields. Come on, you bastard, try another one, he yelled just before the twin-forked purple-mauve bolt twisted down from the front edge of the squall line and tore off the fence at what—in flawed memory—seemed a squared right angle. It hit a bull's-eye on his sternum, so far as the doctors could deduce, leaving a moon-crater burn that never really healed. His father came out shortly to lock up the barn before the storm began (too late), a cheroot lodged in his teeth—and found his son on his back, smoking slightly. During his two-week observational stay in the hospital his teeth ached and sang, although he wouldn't pick up the apocryphal transmissions of those megawatt, over-the-border Mexican radio stations. Upon his return home, Lucy came to his house and—in the silence of a hot summer afternoon—ran her hand down under the band of his BVDs.

∴

Just before the third strike, a few years later, he saw a stubby orphan bolt, a thumb of spark wagging at him from the fence. (Research would later confirm that these microbolts in truth existed.) When *Life* magazine ran a single-page photo montage entitled "Lightning Man," the article said: "Nick Kelley claims he had a strange vision shortly before being struck. He was with two friends in a field a few hours south of Chicago, showing them some property he planned to develop. A small bolt of lightning was seen along a fence just before he was struck. Visions like this, possibly hallucinatory, have been reported by other eyewitnesses." The photo montage showed him in the backyard with a barbecue fork, pointing it at a sky loaded with thick clouds. The report failed to mention the severe contusion along his cheek and certain neurological changes that would reveal themselves over the course of time. His love for Lucy had been obliterated after the second strike. With the third strike his friendship with Danny was vaporized. And in between the first two, he'd temporarily lost all desire to fish.

∴

The fourth had his name on it and was a barn burner, the kind you see locking horns with the Empire State Building. As it came down he talked to it, holding his arms up for an embrace. This was, again, in a boat, out in the middle of Lake Michigan, trolling for coho and steelhead. (He liked the stupid simplicity of fishing in this manner, keeping an eye on the sonar, dragging a downrigger through the depths of the lake, leaning back in his seat, and waiting.) The boat's captain, Pete, caught the edge of the bolt and was burned to a crisp. Nick held a conversation with the big one as he took the full brunt. It went something like this: no matter what, I'll match you, you prick, this story, my story, a hayseed from central Illinois, struck once, twice for good luck, third time, a charm, and now, oh by Jupiter! by Jove! or whatever, oh storm of narrative and calamity. Oh glorious grand design of nature. Rage through me. Grant my heart the guts to resist but not too much. Make me, oh Lord, a good conductor. I will suffer *imitatone Christi*, taking on the burdens of the current and endeavoring to live again.

∴

Shortly after his release from Chicago General, he began weekly attendance of the Second Church of God (or was it the Third?), where he met his first wife, Agnes, who bore an uncanny resemblance to Lucy (same peaches-and-cream complexion). When it came to his past and his history with

4

lightning, scars aside, he had the reticence of a Cold War spy: the book was closed on cloud-to-ground, on hexes, on lightning rod drummers, and the mystical crowd. (He had been offered gigs selling Pro-teck-o-Charge Safe-T rods. LIGHTNING IS THE NO. 1 CAUSE OF BARN FIRES!!!! and from 1-800-Know Your Future.) The book was closed on media interviews, on direct one-on-one confrontations with big bolts. (He in no way worried about smaller variants of lightning, those stray electrical fields that haunt most houses, those freak power surges that melt phone lines and blow phones blank, or those bolts of energy that float bemused into farmhouse windows.) Later he'd come to think that he had been willfully ignoring these forms and thereby picked a fight with them. Once, a film crew from France tracked him down to dredge up the past, but for the most part he urged himself into a normal life and felt bereft of charge, working at the PR firm, representing some commodities brokers, so that when the next strike came it was out of the blue—the blue yonder, a rogue bit of static charge, summer heat lightning. This time he and Agnes were safely ensconced in their summer rental in upstate Michigan watching the Cubs on television. Agnes lay prone on the divan wearing only panties and a bra, exposing her long legs and her school-girl belly and the dimpled muscles of thigh. The cobwebby bolt radiated in a blue antimacassar across the window screen, collected itself, swept through the window, and seemed to congeal around her so that in that brief moment before she was killed, before the power failure plunged the room into black, he was granted a photo negative of her glorious form.

∴

To get away from Chicago, he bought the old family farm, rebuilt the big barn, installing along its roof line six rods with fat blue bulbs attached to thick braided aluminum wires dangling from the barn's sides. The horizon in those parts let the sky win. Even the corn seemed to be hunching low in anticipation of the next strike. In the evenings he read Kant and began dating a woman named Stacy, a large-boned farm widow who dabbled in poetry and quoted from T. S. Eliot, the whole first section of "Ash Wednesday," for example, and entire scenes from *The Cocktail Party*. Nick was fifty now, lean from the fieldwork, with chronic back pain from driving the combine. But he loved the work. He loved the long stretches of being alone in the cab, listening to Mozart sonatas while the corn marched forward into the arch lights, eager to be engulfed by the mawing machine. Behind the cab—in the starlit darkness—emerged the bald swath of landscape.

∴

No more messing around. His days of heady challenge were over, Nick thought, ignoring the pliant flexible nature of lightning itself, the dramatically disjointed manner in which it put itself into the air, the double-jointed way it could defy itself. The Morrison homestead was about as dead out-there as you could get. He was working night and day to harvest the soybeans, trying to compete with the big Iowa industrial farms. Too tired to give a shit. Thunderstorm season was mostly done. Those fall storms that heaved through seemed exhausted and bored with the earth, offering up a pathetic rain, if anything.

∴

The bolt that struck him the sixth time came out from under the veil of the sky—as witnessed by his farmhand, Earl, who was unhitching some equipment and just happened to glance at Nick resting his back in the yellow lawn chair. The whopper bolt struck twenty feet away from Nick, balled itself up, rolled to his feet, and exploded. He flew head over heels against the barn. In the hospital he remembered the medicine ball exercises from grammar school gym class, heaving the leather-clad ball at each other, relishing the absurdity of the game: trying like hell to knock the other guy over, to overcome him with the inertia of the object. To properly catch a medicine ball you had to absorb the force and fall back with it so that at some point both you and the ball's momentum were married to each other. It was a delicate dance. He was pretty good at it.

∴

Nick suffered further neurological damage, strange visions, a sparkling bloom of fireworks under his eyelids. He began to remember. It became clear. He had separated from himself during the strike. A doppelganger of sorts had emerged from his body: a little stoop-shouldered man, thin and frail, making small poking gestures with his cane as he listed forward. A soil sniffer of the old type. A man who could gather up a palm full of dirt and bring it to his nose and give you a rundown of its qualities—moistness and pH and lime content; this was the old dirt farmer of yore who knew his dry-farming methods and gave long intricate dances to the sky urging the beastly drought to come to an end. This man longed more than anything for the clouds to burst open at its seams, for a release of tension in the air, for not just thunder and lightning but the downpour the land deserved. He was a remnant of all those dry-method farmers of yesterday: failed and broken by the land, trying as best they could to find the fix, an old traditional rain dance, or a man who came with a cannon to shoot holes in the sky. Beneath the spot where the lightning ball had landed the soil had fused to glass, and below that—Earl took a shovel and dug it up—the glass extended in an icicle five feet long, branching down to the underground cable that delivered current from the old barn to the storage shed. A power-company representative explained that these underground cables were as prone as aboveground wires to lightning strikes. God knows why, he added.

∴

For three weeks Stacy sat beside his hospital bed and accompanied his anguish by singing odes and folk songs and small ditties she'd picked up as a kid in Alabama, in addition to going through the complete collected poems of Eliot. She had a pure hard voice that seemed carved out of the American soil. In the bandage casing, amid the welts of itching and the

drips of sweat running down his legs—all unreachable loca-
tions—he had acute visions of combat in Korea, the U.S. First
Cavalry Division taking the full brunt of a barrage of Katyusha
rockets—until bolt no. 8 (as he envisioned it) intervened, with
its thick girth, the revoltingly huge embrace of the horizon as
it came eagerly down. It was the big one, the finalization of
several conjoining forks into one, unimaginable fury.

∴

After Stacy took off on him, he put the farm up for sale
and moved six miles to the north. He would live a bach-
elor life in a small Illinois town. A siege mentality had set in.
He would hunker down, avoid fate by immersing himself in
the lackluster flow of the landscape, in the view from his room
over the Ellison Feed & Seed store, a vista so boring it made
you want to spit (and he did). Boarding in the rooms around
him were exiled farm boys who sniffed glue from brown bags,
listened to music, and whiled away days writing on the walls
with Magic Markers. There was nobody as deviant and lost as
an ex–farm boy, he would come to learn. They were depressed
from knowing that the whole concept of the farm—the agrar-
ian mythos of land-human love, not to mention the toil and
tribulation of their own kin, who had suffered dust bowls,
drought, and seed molds—had been reduced to a historical
joke. Industrial farms ruled. Left perplexed in their skin, they
listened to hip-hop, attempted more urbane poses (many had
missing limbs), smoked crack and jimsonweed, stalked the
night half naked in their overalls, carved tattoos into their own

arms. Nick felt akin to them. In their own way, they'd been struck by lightning, too.

∴

Of course the next strike (no. 7) did come. It arrived in a preposterously arrogant manner, in a situation so laden with cliché that even Nick had to laugh it off when he could laugh, weeks later, after the trembles, the delusions, and the spark-filled sideshows. He knew that the next one would be his last. The next one would be the killer. The end. No more after that one. He felt no. 8 at the side of his vision, as he stared out the window at the dead town, so dry—caught in a midsummer drought—it made his throat itch. In his field of vision there now appeared a blank spot, empty and deep and dark. The room crackled in the midsummer heat. The window opened to a view of a defunct farm town, circa 1920, with false-front facades in the Western style, buildings shell-shocked and plucked clean of life. The beaverboard walls grew rank and emitted a dry mustard smell. In the long afternoon shadows the farm boys hung out with crumpled bags to their faces—breathing the glue the way injured grunts took bottled oxygen. As if it made a difference. When he ventured downstairs he walked with a hobble, keeping his weight off the balls of his feet, which were swollen and raw. Now I can safely be called enfeebled, he told the boys. They gathered around him, fingering his scars, showing in kind their own tattoos and flesh wounds, stumps that flicked quickly, glossy twists that traced the half-healed paths of box-cutter slashes and paint-scraper battles. They offered him crumpled bags. He declined. They offered him gasoline to sniff, weed, Valium. They asked him to tell his stories, and he did, giving them long tales, embellishing details at will, watching them nod slowly in appreciation. Here was something they could understand. Nature playing mind games. Nature fucking with him. He dug deep into the nature of lightning. He made himself heroic. He raised his fist like Zeus, catching bolts out of air. He tossed balled lightning, dribbled in for a fast break. This was the least he could do for them. He pitied them for their empty eyes, for the dead slurry way they spoke.

∴

In the dark room as the days turned and the sun raged over the cracked streets below, shrub-size weeds driving up through the damaged macadam, Nick let the siege mentality develop. He would avoid the next one. No. 7 had come just after his complete recovery, when he was called back to Chicago to make a court appearance in litigation over an option fund. He had gone out to the Oak Ridge Country Club with Albert Forster. The club would soon install lightning detection equipment—the first of its kind of the Chicago metro area—to forewarn of exactly the kind of conditions that led to strike no. 7. A mass of cold air arrived from Canada, dug into the hot reaches of the Central Plains, picked up steam, and formed a storm front that had already spawned a classic F-4 tornado, reducing one trailer park to a salad of pink fluffly insulation material, chips of fiberglass, and chunks of Sheetrock. As he teed up on the second hole, bunching his shoulders in a manner that foretold of his forthcoming slice, the front was tonguing into the sticky summer air overhead. In the end it was just another bolt. Simple as that. It appeared as a surprise. Two blunt rumbles swallowed the golf course, a flick behind them, and then, just as Nick threw his club into his backswing, adjusting his shoulders, head cocked, eyes upward on the sky, no. 7 forked down, split into five wayward crabs of raw voltage, and speared him in the brow the way you'd poke a shrimp with a cocktail fork.

∴

In the room he listened to the walls crackle and sat in front of an oscillating metal fan and didn't move for hours at a time. Down the street old Ralph the barber told his own kind of lightning stories about the Battle of the Bulge. If the rotating fan failed to keep him company, he'd go down to watch Ralph cut hair. Outside Ralph's establishment a wooden pole turned to rot. Inside, the mirrors were clean and the chrome and white enamel basins were kept shiny. The sad parameters of his life became nicely apparent at Ralph's. Here is a man defined by lightning, the shop said. Here is a man who could use a shave. A bit off the sides, layered in back. In the shop, his story was lore, it was myth, it was good talk. It was clear in those humble confines, amid the snip of sheers, the concise irreversible nature of cutting hair. (People just don't realize how tough human hair is to cut, Ralph said.) Amid barbering—flattops, Princetons, layer cuts, wet and dry—the best Nick could do was to answer the probing questions that Ralph sent his way. He embellished as much as he could. But he didn't lie. In the barbershop, words felt ponderous and heavy. He filled in with silence as much as he could, and when that didn't work, he hemmed and hawed. But with Ralph the silence seemed necessary. What went unspoken was filled in with Ralph's grunts and his nods and his attention to whoever was getting a cut; if he was between cuts, he might be cleaning the sink or arranging his scissors or stropping his razor with thoughtless Zen strokes. Christ, it's a good story you got, Nick, he said after hearing an account of no. 7. Ralph had a long, pale face— the face of a man who seldom saw the sun—with eyes that drooped in sockets that drooped. Ralph sat on a fence between doubt and belief. He would never fully believe this strange man who came out of the blue and claimed to have owned the Morrison tract, the famous farm over in the next county, a farm that was at one time perhaps the best-run bit of land in that part of Lincoln County. He would only half believe this guy who seemed so weatherworn and odd. Men like this arrived often out of the Great Plains, even now, years after the great wanderings of hobos and tramps, and they often spoke in a reverent voice of preposterous and prophetic events, events that were mostly untrue but that somehow had the ring of truth. Ralph knew the importance of such souls. They walked the line between fact and fiction, and in doing so lightened the load of the truth. They made you aware of the great desolate span of the Central states, of the empty space that still prevailed. He snipped with care around the ears and then snapped the buzzers on and cleaned up the neck, working to create a neat line. He would listen to Lightning Man's stories again, and by the time the man's whole repertoire of tales was used up, another year or so would have passed and he'd be ready to hear them again, forgetting enough of the details to make it interesting. Lightning Man would become a fixture in the shop. He'd have his own chair and ashtray. Into the long afternoons his words would pass. A place would be found for this man. Odd chores would be offered so that he might find subsistence, a few bucks here or there. In this manner another soul would be able to conclude his days upon the earth—at least until the odd premonitions came and the air grew absurdly still and above the shop the clouds began their boiling congregation, and then a faint foreshadowing taste of ozone would arrive. Then everything would change, and nothing would be the same again.

[SAULT STE. MARIE]

Ernie dug in with the tip of his penknife, scratching a line into the plastic top of the display case, following the miniature lock system as it stepped down between Lake Superior and Lake Huron. At the window, Marsha ignored us both and stood blowing clouds of smoke at the vista . . . a supertanker rising slowly in the lock, hefted by water . . . as if it mattered that the system was fully functioning and freight was moving up and down the great seaway. As if it mattered that ore was being transported from the hinterlands of Duluth (a nullifyingly boring place) to the eastern seaboard and points beyond. As if it mattered that the visitor's center stood bathed in sunlight, while behind the gift counter an old lady sat reading a paperback and doing her best to ignore the dry scratch of Ernie's knife, raising her rheumy eyes on occasion, reaching

15

up to adjust her magnificent hair with the flat of her hand.
—I'm gonna go see that guy I know, Tull, about the boat I was
telling you about, Ernie announced, handing me the knife. He
tossed his long black hair to the side, reached into his pants,
yanked out his ridiculously long-barreled .44 Remington
Magnum, pointed it at the lady, and said, —But first I'm going to rob this old bag. —Stick 'em up, he said, moving toward
the lady who stared over the top of her paperback. Her face
was ancient; the skin drooped from her jaw, and on her chin
bits of hair collected faintly into something that looked like a
Vandyke. A barmaid beauty remained in her face, along with
a stony resilience. Her saving feature was a great big poof of
silvery hair that rose like a nest and stood secured by an
arrangement of bobby pins and a very fine hairnet. —Take
whatever you want, she said in a husky voice, lifting her hands
out in a gesture of offering. —As a matter of fact, shoot me if
you feel inclined. It's not going to matter to me. I'm pushing
eighty. I've lived the life I'm going to live and I've seen plenty
of things and had my heart broken and I've got rheumatoid
arthritis in these knuckles so bad I can hardly hold a pencil to
paper. (She lifted her hand so we could see the claw formation
of her fingers.) —And putting numbers into the cash register
is painful. —Jesus Christ, Ernie said, shooting you would just
be doing the world a favor, and too much fun, and he tucked
the gun back in his pants, adjusted the hem of his shirt, and
went to find this guy with the boat. Marsha maintained her
place at the window, lit another cigarette, and stared at the
boat while I took Ernie's knife from the top of the display case

and began scratching where he left off. Finished with the matter, the old lady behind the gift counter raised the paperback up to her face and began reading. Outside, the superfreighter rose with leisure; it was one of those long ore boats, a football field in length, with guys on bicycles making the journey from bow to stern. There was probably great beauty in its immensity, in the way it emerged from the lower parts of the seaway, lifted by the water. But I didn't see it. At that time in my life, it was just one more industrial relic in my face.

∴

A few minutes later, when Ernie shot the guy named Tull in the parking lot, the gun produced a tight little report that bounced off the side of the freighter that was sitting up in the lock, waiting for the go-ahead. The weight line along the ship's hull was far above the visitor's station; below the white stripe, the skin of the hull was shoddy with flakes of rust and barnacle scars. The ship looked ashamed of itself exposed for the whole world to see, like a lady with her skirt blown up. The name on the bow, in bright white letters, was Henry Jackman. Looking down at us, a crew member raised his hand against the glare. What he saw was a sad scene: a ring of blue gun smoke lingering around the guy Ernie shot, who was muttering the word fuck and bowing down while blood pooled around his crotch. By the time we scrambled to the truck and got out of there, he was trembling softly on the pavement, as if he were trying to limbo-dance under an impossibly low bar. I can assure you now, the guy didn't die that morning. A year later we came face-to-face at an amusement park near Bay City, and he looked perfectly fine, strapped into a contraption that would—a few seconds after our eyes met— roll him into a triple corkscrew at eighty miles an hour. I like to imagine that the roller coaster ride shook his vision of me into an aberration that stuck in his mind for the rest of his earthly life.

∴

For what it's worth, the back streets of Sault Ste. Marie, Michigan, were made of concrete with nubs of stone mixed in, crisscrossed with crevices, passing grand old homes fallen to disrepair—homes breathing the smell of mildew and dry rot from their broken windows. Ernie drove with his hand up at the noon position while the police sirens wove through the afternoon heat behind us. The sound was frail, distant, and meaningless. We'd heard the same thing at least a dozen times in the past three weeks, from town to town, always respect- fully distant, unraveling, twisting around like a smoke in a breeze until it disappeared. Our river of luck was deep and fed by an artesian well of fate. Ernie had a knack for guiding us out of bad situations. We stuck up a convenience store, taking off with fifty bucks and five green-and-white cartons of men- thol cigarettes. Then a few days later we hog-tied a liquor store clerk and made off with a box of Cutty Sark and five rolls of Michigan Scratch-Off Lotto tickets. Under Ernie's leadership, we tied up our victims with bravado, in front of the fish-eyed video monitors, our heads in balaclavas. We put up the V sign and shouted: Liberation for all! For good measure, we turned to the camera and yelled: Patty Hearst lives! The next morning the *Detroit Free Press* Sunday edition carried a photo, dramatically smudgy, of the three us bent and rounded off by the lens, with our guns in the air. The accompanying article speculated on our significance. According to the article, we were a highly disciplined group with strong connections to California, our gusto and verve reflecting a nationwide resurgence of Weathermen-type radicals. —A place to launch the boat will provide itself, Ernie said, sealing his lips around his dangling cigarette and pulling in smoke. Marsha rooted around in the glove box and found a flaying knife, serrated and brutal-looking, with a smear of dried blood on the oak handle. She handed it to me, dug around some more, and found a baggie with pills, little blue numbers; a couple of bright reds, all mystery and portent. She spun it around a few times and then gave out a long yodel that left our ears tingling. Marsha was a champion yodeler. Of course we popped the pills and swallowed them dry while Ernie raged through the center of town, running two red lights, yanking the boat behind us like an afterthought. Marsha had her feet on the dash and her hair tangled beautifully around her eyes and against her lips. It was the best feeling in the world to be running from the law with a boat in tow, fishtailing around corners, tossing our back wheels into the remnants of the turn, rattling wildly over the potholes, roaring through a shithole town that was desperately trying to stay afloat in the modern world and finding itself sinking deeper into squalor beneath a sky that unfurled blue and deep. All this along with drugs that were swiftly going about their perplexing work, turning the whole show inside out and making us acutely aware of the fact that above all we were nothing much more than a collection of raw sensations. Marsha's legs emerging beautiful from her fringed cutoff shorts—the shorts are another story—and her bare toes, with her nails painted cherry red, wiggled in the breeze from the windows. The seaway at the bottom of the street, spread out in front of a few lonely houses, driftwood gray, rickety and grand, baking in the summer heat. They crackled with dryness. They looked ready to explode into flames. They looked bereft of all hope. In front of a Victorian, a single dog, held taut by a long length of rope, barked and tried to break free, turning and twisting and looping the full circumference of his plight. We parked across the street, got out of the truck, and looked at him while he, in turn, looked back. He was barking SOS. Over and over again. Bark bark bark. Bark bark bark. Bark bark bark. Bark bark bark. Bark bark bark. Until finally Ernie yanked his gun from his belt, pointed quickly, with both hands extended out for stability, and released a shot that materialized as a burst of blooming dust near the dog; then another shot that went over his head and splintered a porch rail. The dog stopped barking and the startled air glimmered, got brighter, shiny around the edges, and then fell back into the kind of dull haze you find only in small towns in summer, with no one around but a dog who has finally lost the desire to bark. The dog sat staring at us. He was perfectly fine but stone-still. Out in the water a container ship stood with solemnity, as if dumb-

founded by its own passage, covered in bright green tarps.
—We're gonna drop her right here, Ernie said, unleashing the
boat, throwing back restraining straps, trying to look like he
knew what he was doing. The water was a five-foot fall from
the corrugated steel and poured cement buttress of the wall.
The Army Corps of Engineers had constructed a breakwall of
ridiculous proportions. We lifted the hitch, removed it from
the ball, and wiggled the trailer over so that the bow of the
boat hung over the edge. Then without consultation—working
off the mutual energies of our highs—we lifted the trailer and
spilled the boat over the edge. It landed in the water with a
plop, worked hard to right itself, coming to terms with its new
place in the world, settling back as Ernie applied the rope and
urged it along to some ladder rungs. To claim this was anything but a love story would be to put Sault Ste. Marie in a
poor light. The depleted look in the sky and the sensation of
the pills working in our bloodstreams, enlivening the water,
the slap and pop of the metal hull over the waves. The superfreighter (the one with green tarps) looming at our approach.
To go into those details too much would be to bypass the es-
sential fact of the matter. I was deeply in love with Marsha.
Nothing else in the universe mattered. I would have killed for
her. I would have swallowed the earth like an egg-eating
snake. I would have turned inside out in my own skin. I was
certain that I might have stepped from the boat and walked on
the water, making little shuffling movements, conserving my
energy, doing what Jesus did but only better. Jesus walked on
water to prove a point. I would have done it for the hell of it.

Just for fun. To prove my love. Up at the bow Ernie stood with his heel on the gunwale, one elbow resting on a knee, looking like the figurehead on a Viking ship. I sat in the back with Marsha, watching as she held the rubber grip and guided the motor with her suspiciously well-groomed fingers. I could see in the jitteriness of her fingers that she was about to swing the boat violently to the side. Maybe not as some deeply mean-spirited act, but just as a joke on Ernie, who was staring straight ahead, making little hoots, patting his gun, and saying, —We're coming to get you. We're gonna highjack us a moth-erfucking superfreighter, boys. I put my hand over Marsha's and held it there. Her legs, emerging out of the fringed grip of her tight cutoff jeans, were gleaming with spray. (She'd am-putated the pants back in a hotel in Manistee, laying them over her naked thighs while we watched, tweaking the loose threads out to make them just right.) Tiny beads of water clung to the downy hairs along the top of her thighs, fringed with her cutoff jeans, nipping and tucking up into her crotch. Who knows? Maybe she was looking at my legs, too, stretched against her own, the white half-moon of my knees poking through the holes in my jeans. When I put my hand over hers I felt our forces conjoin into a desire to toss Ernie overboard.

∴

Two nights later we were alone in an old motel, far up in the nether regions of the Upper Peninsula, near the town of Houghton, where her friend Charlene had ODed a few years back. Same hotel, exactly. Same room, too. She'd persuaded me that she had to go and hold a wake for her dead friend. (—I gotta go to the same hotel, she said. —The same room.) The hotel was frequented mainly by sailors, merchant marine types, a defiled place with soggy rank carpet padding and dirty towels. In bed we finished off a few of Tull's pills. Marsha was naked, resting on her side as she talked to me in a solemn voice about Charlene and how much they had meant to each other one summer, and how, when her own father was on a rage, they would go hide out near the airport, along the fence out there, hanging out and watching the occasional plane arrive, spinning its propellers wildly and making tipping wing gestures as if in a struggle to conjure the elements of flight. Smoking joints and talking softly, they poured out secrets the way only stoner girls can—topping each other's admissions, one after the other, matter-of-factly saying yeah, I did this guy who lived in Detroit and was a dealer and he, like, he like was married and we took his car out to the beach and spent two days doing it. Listening to her talk, it was easy to imagine the two of them sitting out there in the hackweed and elderberry on cooler summer nights, watching the silent airstrips, cracked and neglected, waiting for the flight from Chicago. I'd spent my own time out in that spot. It was where Marsha and I figured out that we were bound by coincidence: our fathers had both worked to their deaths in the paint booth at Fisher Body, making sure the enamel was spread evenly, suffering from the gaps in their masks, from inhaled solvents, and from producing quality automobiles.

∴

I was naked on the bed with Marsha, slightly buzzed, but not stoned out of my sense of awareness. I ran my hand along her hip and down into the concave smoothness of her waist while she, in turn, reached around and pawed and cupped my ass, pulling me forward against her as she cried softly in my ear, just wisps of breath, about nothing in particular except that we were about to have sex. I was going to roll her over softly, expose her ass, find myself against her, and then press my lips to her shoulder blades as I sank in. When I got there, I became aware of the ashen cinder-block smell of the hotel room, the rubber of the damp carpet padding, the walls smeared with mildew, and the large russet stains that marked the dripping zone inside the tub and along the upper rim of the toilet. Outside, the hotel—peeling pink stucco, with a pale blue slide curling into an empty pool—stood along an old road, a logging route, still littered with the relics of a long-past tourist boom. The woods across from the place were thick with undergrowth, and the gaps between trees seemed filled with the dark matter of interstellar space. When we checked in it was just past sunset, but the light was already drawn away by the forest. It went on for miles and miles. Just looking at it too long would be to get lost, to wander in circles. You could feel the fact that we were far up along the top edge of the United States; the north pole began its pull around there, and the aurora borealis spread across the sky. I like to think that we both came out of our skin, together, in one of those orgasmic unifications. I like to think that two extremely lonely souls—both fearing that they had just killed another human being—united themselves carnally for some wider, greater sense of the universe; I like to think that maybe for one moment in my life, I reached up and ran my hand through God's hair. But who knows? Who really knows? The truth remains lodged back in that moment, and that moment is gone, and all I can honestly attest to is that we did feel a deep affection for our lost comrade Ernie at the very moment we were both engaged in fornication. (That's the word Ernie used: I'd like to fornicate with that one over there, or I'm going to find me some fornication.) We lay on the bed and let the breeze come through the hotel window—cool and full of yellow pine dust—across our damp bellies. The air of northern Michigan never quite matches the freshness of Canada. There's usually a dull iron ore residue in it, or the smell of dead flies accumulating between the stones on shore. Staring up at the ceiling, Marsha felt compelled to talk about her dead friend. She lit a smoke and took a deep inhalation and let it sift from between her teeth. (I was endlessly attracted to the big unfixed gap tooth space between her two front ones.) Here's the story she told me in as much detail as I can muster: Charlene was a hard-core drifter, born in Sarnia, Ontario, across the lake from Port Huron. Her grandmother on her mother's side raised her, except for a few summers—the ones in our town—with her deranged auto-worker father. She was passed on to her grandfather on her father's side for some reason, up in Nova Scotia. Her grandfather was an edgy, hard drinker who abused her viciously. Along her ass were little four-leaf-clover scar formations. She ran away from her grandfather, back to her grandmother in Sarnia, and then ran away from her and crossed the International Bridge to Detroit, where she hooked up with a guy named Stan, a maintenance worker at a nursing home, who fixed air conditioners and cleared dementia-plugged toilets. Stan was into cooking crank in his spare time. They set up a lab in a house near Dearborn, in a pretty nice neighborhood, actually. Then one day there was an explosion and Stan got a face full of battery acid. She left him behind and hooked up with another cooker, named King, who had a large operation in a house near Saginaw. She worked with him and helped out, but she never touched the stuff and was angelic and pious about it. Even King saw a kind of beauty in Charlene's abstinence, Marsha said. For all the abuse she had suffered she had a spiritual kind of calm. Her eyes were, like, this amazingly deep blue color. Aside from her scars and all, she still had the whitest, purest skin, Snow White skin, the kind that you just want to touch, like a cool smooth stone. She just got more and more beautiful until eventually the guy named King couldn't stand the gentleness in her eyes and, maybe to try to change things around, he started to beat her face like a punching bag. One afternoon, under the influence of his own product, he had a couple of friends hold her down while he struck her face with a meat pounder, just hammered it, until she was close to death—maybe actually dead. Maybe she left her body and floated above herself and looked down and saw a guy with long shaggy hair and a silver meat hammer bashing her face in and decided it just wasn't worth dying in that kind of situation and so went back into her body. (Marsha was pretty firm in her belief about this part.) Charlene's cheekbones were broken, her teeth shattered. It took about twenty operations on her jaw and teeth just to chew again. Even then, chewing never felt right; her fake teeth slipped from the roof of her mouth, she talked funny, and a ringing sounded in her ears when she tried to smile. When she laughed too hard, her mouth would clamp up and she'd hear a chiming sound, high in pitch, like bells, and then the sound of windswept rain, or wind in a shell, or wind through guy wires, or a dry, dusty windswept street, or the rustling of tissue paper, or a sizzling like a single slice of bacon in a pan, or a dial tone endlessly unwinding in her eardrum. Forever she was up over herself looking down, watching King go at her, the two guys holding on to her shoulders, her legs scissor-kicking, the flash of the hammer until it was impossible to know what was going on beneath the blood. When Marsha met her again—a year or so later, in the break room at Wal-Mart—she had this weirdly deranged face; the out-of-place features demanded some thought to put straight. I mean it was a mess, Marsha said. Her nose was folded over. The Detroit team of plastic and oral surgeons just couldn't put poor Charlene back together again. A total Humpty Dumpty. No one was going to spend large amounts of money on a face of a drifter, anyway. Marsha forced herself to look. Then Charlene told her the story of King, the reasons for the damage, and the whole time Marsha didn't remove her eyes from the nose, the warped cheeks, the fishlike mouth. She tried as hard as she could to see where the beauty had gone and what Charlene must've been like before King mashed her face, the

angelic part, because she kind of doubted her on that aspect of
the story. As far as she could remember, from their nights together getting stoned outside the airport fence, Charlene had
been, well, just a normal-looking kid. But listening to her talk,
she put the pieces together and saw that, yeah, yeah, yeah,
maybe this mishmash of features had once been beautiful. Her
eyes were certainly bright blue, and wide, and she had pale
milky skin. That night after work they decided to go out together, not to a bar where she'd get hassled but just to buy
some beer and go to Charlene's apartment and drink. She had
some little pills she called goners, good God goners, something
like that. So they went to her apartment, took the pills, drank
some beer, and decided to watch *Blue Velvet*. Whatever transpired next, according to Marsha, was amazing and incredibly
sensual; they were stoned together, watching the movie, and
suddenly between them there grew a hugely powerful sense of
closeness; when Marsha looked down at her on the couch,
Charlene appeared to her too gorgeous not to kiss (that's how
she put it, exactly). Her mouth was funny because her teeth
were out, so it was just softness and nothing else and then,
somehow, they undressed—I mean it wasn't like a first for
either of us, Marsha said—and she fell down between
Charlene's knees, and drove her to come, and then they spent
the night together. A few days later, Charlene quit her job and
split for Canada, back over the bridge, and then the next thing
Marsha heard she was up north at this hotel with some guys
and then she ODed.

∴

The story—and the way she told it to me, early in the morning, just before dawn—as both of us slid down from our highs, our bodies tingling and half asleep, turned me on in a grotesque way. To get a hard-on based on a story of abuse seemed wrong, but it happened, and we made love to each other again for the second time, and we both came wildly and lay there for a while until she made her confession. —I made that up, completely. I never knew a drifter named Charlene from Canada, and I certainly wouldn't sleep with a fuckface reject like that. No way. I just felt like telling a story. I felt like making one up for you. I thought it would be interesting and maybe shed some light on the world. The idea—the angelic girl, the perfect girl, the one with perfect beauty getting all mashed up like that. That's something I think about a lot. She sat up, smoking a cigarette, stretching her legs out. Dawn was breaking outside. I imagined the light plunging through the trees, and the log trucks roaring past. For a minute I felt like knocking her on the head. I imagined pinning her down and giving her face a go with a meat hammer. But I found it easy to forgive her because the story she made up had sparked wild and fanciful sex. I kissed her and looked into her eyes and no- ticed that they were sad and didn't move away from mine (but that's not what I noticed). What did I notice? I can't put words to it except to say she had an elegiac sadness there, and an un- earned calm, and that something had been stolen from her pupils. —You weren't making that up, I said. —You couldn't make that shit up, she responded, holding her voice flat and cold. —So it was all true. —I didn't say that. I just said you couldn't make that shit up.

∴

—We're gonna get nailed for what we did, she said, later, as we ate breakfast. Around us truckers in their long-billed caps leaned into plates of food, clinking the heavy silverware, devouring eggs in communal silence. A waitress was dropping dirty dishes into the slop sink, lifting each of them up and letting them fall, as if to test the durability of high-grade, restaurant-quality plates. —We're gonna get nailed, I agreed. I wasn't up for an argument about it. The fact was, our stream of luck would go on flowing for a while longer. Then I'd lose Marsha and start searching for a Charlene. For its part, the world could devour plenty of Ernies; each day they vaporized into the country's huge horizon. —He's probably dead. He knew how to swim, but he didn't look too confident in his stroke. —Yeah, I agreed. Ernie had bobbed up to the surface shouting profanities and striking out in our direction with a weird sidestroke. His lashing hands sustained just his upper body. The rest was sunken out of sight and opened us up to speculation as to whether his boots were on or off. After he was tossed from the boat, he stayed under a long, long time. When he bobbed up, his face had a wrinkled, babyish look of betrayal. He blew water at us, cleared his lips, and in a firm voice said, —You're dead, man, both of you. Then he cursed my mother and father and the day they were born, Marsha's cunt and her ass and her mother and father and God and the elements and the ice-cold water of the seaway and the ship, which was about four hundred yards away (—come on, motherfuckers, save my ass). He kept shouting like this until a mouth full of water gagged him. We were swinging around, opening it up full-throttle, looping around, sending a wake in his direction and heading in. When we got to the breakwall we turned and saw that he was still out there, splashing, barely visible. The ship loomed stupidly in the background, oblivious to his situation. A single gull spiraled overhead, providing us with an omen to talk about later. (Gulls are God's death searchers, Marsha told me. Don't be fooled by their white feathers or any of that shit. Gulls are best at finding the dead.) We got back in Tull's truck and headed through town and out, just following roads north toward Houghton, leaving Ernie to whatever destiny he had as one more aberration adrift in the St. Lawrence Seaway system. For a long time we didn't say a word. We just drove. The radio was playing a Neil Young song. We turned it up, and then up some more, and left it loud like that, until it was just so much rattling noise, a high nasal twang caught in a cyclone of distortion.

[IT COUNTS AS SEEING]

I went right up to him and took his elbow, not even asking him if I should because he was heading hellfire for the first step, not seeing—because how could he?—that step, flashing his red-tipped cane around in the air (*in the air*, I stress). What else could I do except grab him? Others might have gone for his hand or shoulder, but having been trained in the proprieties of guiding the blind, I took the back of his elbow, which he jerked quickly away before stating, flatly, in a firm, resolute manner, with a slight accent—British or mock British, at least Harvard—back off. Back off, he says, and I let go and then he tumbles all the way down to the bottom of the stairs, doing this cartwheel motion, head over heels. He had a firm grasp on the acrobatics of his tumble, I think, and when it slowed down in my mind it was very much like those folks up in space goofing off, showing the schmucks down on earth, poor souls, the delights of zero-G. This blind guy took a prim and proper control of his body in relation to gravity and went down those stairs with wild agility, not a bone broken or a ligament torn in this version of events. Across the street people looked wild-eyed at the scene. One gentleman—in an elegant suit coat and tie—I noticed specifically, a witness, who would back up my claim (or so I thought at the time) that I was only trying to assist this blind guy in getting down the stairs. This man made a beeline across the street and stepped over the moaning blind man and came right up and began to shout. He had a ruddy face, up close, with pockmarks, a drinker's face, my father would say, and this face ruined the suit coat. Up close it was stained with glossy streaks of what look like melted butter. This quick assessment made me realize that he was a derelict who, along with one other guy in town, slept in doorways, copped a buck here and there, and so on and so forth. I realized that he didn't witness the fall, and was yelling at me about something else, had me pegged for someone else, apparently, and was yelling, —Marvin, you're going to have to spare me this kind of aggravation, you bastard, because for God's sake, Mary is not going to leave you for me, or me for you, or any of that. I didn't see the blind guy at all before he hit that first step, until he was already falling. I was in the bank shuffling through my withdrawal—new twenties, still crisp and unbroken and therefore impossible to get apart. I was trying to part them and walk at the same time—around me the hollow cacophony of the marble, real marble from the days of real banks—when out of the edge of my eye, not the corner, through the bright front doors, bathed in midday light, really, really bright, I saw the blind guy (I had noticed him ahead of me in the line and wondered how he might find his way to the proper window, or the exact place in front of the window, noting that the cashier gave him slight directions, a bit to your right, a bit to your left, sir—until lined up in the correct trajectory, he moved forward), but then I was beckoned to my window and went up and put the check into the little metal throat and forgot about the blind guy until I was back by the door counting the cash and saw him take that step into what must have been, surprisingly, empty space. His heels went skyward, rubber tennis shoes, those white clunking sneakers you see old folks wearing, and then he was out of my vision and I had a moment's pause: in that moment I recollected that the blind man was named Harrington and that he was made blind (is that the proper term?) in a freak flash fire on his yacht when he was spreading sealing putty and the vapors ignited. He was owner of the boatyard down the river and had an estate near there, too. When I got out to the steps a crowd was gathering around, stepping carefully to avoid the pool of dark blood around his head. For some reason I stood unwilling to commit myself to going down the steps, and in that moment a girl—maybe fourteen or twenty (it's hard for me to differentiate between ages of these kids)—glanced at me. Our eyes met, as they say. Hers were hazy and dark, maybe hazel-colored. She drew forth her hand and pointed her finger like a pistol and said, loudly, He pushed him. I saw that fucker push the guy. That asshole shoved the blind man down the stairs. Before I could move I was beset upon from behind by two burly men, both with security guard uniforms and fake sheriff badges. They put me into a proper headlock and secured my wrists with cuffs.

∴

I swell with a solicitous desire to help the blind man tick tick ticking his way ahead of me out of the bank, with an almost imperative desire to help at all costs, no matter what his needs. No question about it, I'm going to help him through the doors and out and into the street after properly guiding him down the stairs. Counting my bills, fanning the crisp ones out, at the same time closing in on the guy, all the while also searching memory banks for more information on the blind man, putting together fragments of gossip—the owner of that boat with the fire, his house clearly available to my mind's eye, wondrously large, situated on about five acres of expensive land stretching in wide vistas of rolled lawn all the way down to the river. Almost ready to burst with the desire not only to take his elbow but to touch it, too, to feel the sharp (is there a sharper, more protruding object in the human body?) bony nub of it in my hands, and to help him down the walk whether he wants it or not. No matter what his feelings are on the matter, I'm bound by some deeper internal duty to help him out and in doing so, of course, as will be pointed out to me later, after the fall, when his blood is pooling around his head, to help myself out as well by satisfying my compulsion to help.

∴

My desire to help guide the blind man when I see him through the bank doors is just tiny, nothing much, a very small seed in the core of my fruitless heart. Microscopic is the way I describe it to the police during the inquest into the fall and the so-called riotous aftermath. Not duty or a sense of right and wrong but maybe a small hint that if I do not help this man who is swaying toward that fateful first step, then in some way I will be indicted as *one who did not come to the aid of a fellow human,* no matter how sordid or pathetic that human might be, which was the case, because this man stank of urine and God knows what—dirty from top to bottom. This image of his face stuck with me through the whole process: here was a man with a fine estate and with so much to his name, putting aside the damage he suffered in that horrible fire, who has let himself go to seed. His face was not only blemished by the scar tissue, which would be expected in such cases, but was also dirty in an industrial sense, with grit and grime and smears of what seemed to be axle grease smashed into his pores. Coming upon him and trying to take hold of the very fine nub of his elbow, bony and sharp, I thought of that Walker Evans photo: a man in the moth-holed cap presumably just out of the coal mine, clutching his shovel handle, staring half blankly into the lens. Not a bit of charm or irony on that fucked-up face. A face void of insight. A blank face holding all the blank portents of humankind. The blind man's face was similar but gave the impression that it might be cleaned up with a good scrubbing: just a nail brush and a bar of lava soap. My desire was only to clean up this man, to move him toward some place where he might be able to bathe, to rub his back with a brush, to scrub beneath his nails, to shave, to buff his feet with a pumice stone, to shampoo his scalp, to dab a cloth under the fold of his ears, to sprinkle aftershave across his face, to trim his nose hairs, to pluck his brows, to clip his nails, to exfoliate his skin, to brush his shiny hair; a desire to move him at least in the direction of all this had me slightly ahead of the blind man, nudging him and therefore causing him to misstep and tumble forward. Unfortunate as it is, the story does have its elements of humor, I am told: the acrobatic, clownish nature of his fall. His foppish Chaplinesque bowlegged tramp moves as he fell. The whole thing is certainly grist for the rumor mill. Many are afloat regarding the event: I pushed him./ I was angry and insisted that I help him./ I didn't help him./ I didn't come near him./ I was still in the bank counting my money when he fell./ I gave him a good hard kick in the ass./ He staged the whole event in order to sue me./ He was suicidal and found the most intricate manner to kill himself—so intricate he could not have planned it in such detail./ He pushed me./ I pushed him back./ We pushed each other and fell simultaneously./ He wasn't blind./ He was a fraud./ I was the one who was blind—legally, though I could see colorless masses across my field of vision./ I wasn't near the bank. I was in the Grand Union.

∴

When I came out of the bank the blind man was being hoisted into the ambulance, one of those boxy affairs, more a truck than the kind we used to have, which were low and sleek station wagons, making me aware, on seeing the man being hoisted in, that the hearse, a direct relative to the ambulance, hasn't kept up with the evolution of styles, or else has stayed back in the past for some good reason. A blind man is being put into the ambulance, I thought, because one of the EMS technicians had put his cane neatly alongside of him, though not under the blanket but next to the man and held down by the Velcro straps. The blood was clearly evident, and I heard talk near me of what had happened, that the man had taken a tumble, had fallen head over heels, someone said, no kidding, actually did a little somersault/cartwheel on the way down, you should've seen it, this blind guy comes out and this other guy comes behind him to help and it looks, well, it looks as if this man gives him a push instead of helping, and then next thing you know the blind guy's falling. Down amid the crowd I spot blue shirts, badges, notepads out, a man in handcuffs, or not cuffs but those little elastic straps they use when they arrest a bunch of people at once, demonstrators and the like, mass arrests more than anything, but sometimes used instead of handcuffs to avoid the stigma of metal cuffs; this very elegant man in a fine suit coat and a tie, thin, maybe gaunt, very European-looking, I think, a slightly bewildered look on his face, eyeing the crowd as it closed in on him with ears cocked (if ears can cock) to hear his side of the story, and he's looking through the crowd right at me, and we exchange what seems to be a kind of knowing glance, though I've never seen him before, I don't think, not sure, doing a search of my memory because in this town you mostly know everybody. I don't know him. I'm pretty sure I've never seen him before. But to be sure, I get a bit closer, shoving through the crowd, and get up near him and see that he is a very dainty man, very refined up close with a very thin veneer of sweat over his whole face, from top to bottom. He nods in a knowing way that says he somehow recognizes me, too, and is going through his own mental records to try to make the connection. But before he can speak—because his mouth is open—he is whisked away, held on both sides by the cops who have to get him through the crowd, which is closing in, a few people shouting and calling him an asshole and saying he should be shot, pushing a blind man down stairs like that, until out of impulse I am shouting at him, too, going with it, yelling, You're the most vile bastard on the face of the earth, how dare you push a poor soul down the stairs, a blind man no less, blind as a bat, blind as Lear, how can such evil be allowed to coexist with all the good things of this earth? And so on and so forth as I work my way as close to him as I can, so that I'm hanging over him, right behind the cop, as he's forced down into the car seat, though he isn't resisting at all.

∴

After making a deposit of berth fees for my boatyard, I'm going as usual out the bank to the steps, feeling the nub of my cane hitting the first void (that's the word I use for any place where the cane refuses touch, comes up empty-handed, so to speak), not thinking, of course, because all this touch-and-feel stuff is second nature to me—translating the taps, vibrations up the cane to my hand and in turn into my brain, where the sensation is translated to the dimensions of space. And, in any case, I know the bank steps well from years of using them pre–sight loss, nothing to it, six wide stairs of—what? Not marble, maybe sandstone—and just as I'm to the first step, feeling for the drop, this hand takes my elbow and a voice says behind me, Let me. I push back slightly, saying Back off, because I hate help most of the time and especially when I know the place and layout and have the whole thing premapped in my head, yet even more so when it's a clammy hand on me, a sopping wet palm. Then next thing I'm going through the air and there's an explosive flowering of sparks in my eyelids (a classic flowering of sparks, probably from the pressure of the brain striking so violently against the cerebral sac), or not so much the eyelids but back near the center of my brain. Then I'm being transported to the hospital, waking to the jitters of bad truck shocks over the potholed main streets (another ability one learns with sight loss is naming streets based on pothole thuds and thumps and various brands of pavement and blacktop—there is a shocking inconsistency in the various grades of paving materials, a conspiracy of gradients), feeling on my way to the hospital partly used and violated because there is still a cold sort of faint impression on my elbow, the point where I think the man touched me—and his voice is hovering in my ear, that Let me. And then I'm being tended in critical care, hardly hanging on, with severe hemorrhaging (I'm told later) and a very bad contusion along my temple.

Near-death experiences abound. I'm angelic. I'm lifted through the joists and beams of the hospital and am flying out over the town. I'm fully vested with sight. The Hudson is fantastically blue. It hooks to the west near Indian Point, the domes of the power plant spewing steam. To the south through the milky haze of a summer day is the thin gray conjoined monolith of the World Trade Center on the horizon; and to the left of it, the needle point of the Empire State Building injecting the sky. Holy. Holy. Holy. I'm vested with visions. I see it all.

It is this vision alone that has sustained me through it all, kept me alive. It is this vision—because it was so good and pure—that I count as actually seeing. It makes me want to thank the man who helped me down those steps, to offer him my hand, to plant a check for at least a thousand dollars in his hands. It is true that before the fire rose up to take my eyes I was so used to seeing the open vistas of the Hudson that I hardly knew I was seeing them and took for granted the simple sight of the Westchester shore. Sailing a boat itself is an extremely visual experience, much more than people would ever imagine: the luffing sails always in need of trimming, those small little wavelet ripples along the taut cloth near the top of the mast, the heeling of the boat against the horizon.

∴

This blind guy was just about to take a tumble—I mean quivering right over the edge of the steps, not even bothering with his cane, tucking it up under his armpit, because he was using both hands to stuff some bills back into the narrow bank envelope and was having a hard time because the bills were soft and finger-worn, like a sow's ear (or as soft as chamois). He was approaching the steps a bit sidelong, just about to the steep and narrow risers—built to look grand and stately when seen from the street. Being versed in architectonics, an engineer expert in spotting structural deficiencies, I noticed the disharmony in the whole setup, which included this man who was going toward the steps as I moved about two yards behind him. Then he did a frozen midair poise, a stasis, holding there, his seersucker suit wrinkled around his hips, a big stain of yellow across the back of the coat (one of those stains that appear when you pull the coat, reeking of moth flakes, out of winter storage). I knew the man not by name but by his reputation as the owner of the old boatyard, who had suffered from a freak accident (according to some) or by foolishness (according to others), spackling down a gluing compound while igniting a Camel Light and thereby creating a massive cloud of dull blue flame that devoured his boat and his eyesight. As a divorcé (everyone knew), he carried a lonely demeanor along with his blindness; by this I mean beside his blindness or compounded by it. You could tweeze this aspect out of him if you tried hard, separate it the way a prism might separate light, so that you knew his wife, Janice, who had remarried and might be seen picking her kid up from the front of school at times, hadn't just left him because of the blindness (you gave her the grace of that doubt) and probably had left him for much better and clear-cut reasons, one of which was his nasty temper. He was seen taking a hammer to the last of his boats, a blue-trimmed day cruiser—blindly groping his way over the hull and smashing the bulkhead before one of his yard hands grabbed him from behind and subdued him. Rumor has it that it took at least five men to get him calmed down. He fought like a man who couldn't see, clawing the air with his fists, kicking whatever he could, clutching whatever was there to grab. Perhaps this gave me pause, this violent tendency—or the hearsay of it, the rumor itself solidifying into something larger than this man. Rumor also had it that he hated like hell to be helped in any manner and was prone to taking his cane to the side of your head if you did so much as offer up a careful hand on the elbow, and had even fought valiantly against a warning device to help guide the sight-impaired across the streets of our fair town. The fear that he might slam his cane into my brow restrained me. I did nothing. I waited half a second and let him take that step. I did give a bit of a warning shout, just before he went down. It was a squeak, my wife said, like air being released through the taut neck of a balloon. Off he went into the air, head over heels. My shoes felt heavy on the steps. I went down and cradled his heavy head and stated firmly that someone should call 911. You're not going to hit me with your cane, I was thinking, you're not going to hurt anyone. But I was saying, You're gonna be all right, pal. It's going to be all right buddy. You ain't slipping away from us yet. Hang in there. Hang on. Help is on the way. It'll be here soon. Don't move. Don't move at all. Just stay right there and breathe easy. Take nice easy breaths. Don't go. Don't go at all. Just a few minutes and you'll be on your way.

BLOWN FROM
THE BRIDGE

A small car had blown from the bridge. He heard it in a news report, but when it happened, exactly, he can't remember—and now it's like any old news report, nothing but a premonition. A small Toyota compact was swept from the bridge during one of three days of high winds. (This was back when small Japanese-built cars were a novelty, and many in Michigan shrugged and said, "See what buying one of those little tin shit cans will do to you?")

A fine drift of snow moved over the meeting point of two massive, surging bodies of water; it covered the lurking currents. He imagined the car floating down, making a swan dive into the icy reaches.

Those currents battling each other between two great lakes at the Straits of Mackinac, pounding past St. Ignace, surging along Nine Mile Point. Into this unimaginable fury of currents she falls, angelic with her hair lifting up and her face settled into terror and then grace (it's five or so seconds before she hits the water) or whatever you want to call it as for the first time, perhaps in years, she becomes completely placid, almost joyous. The car hits the choppy foam and lingers upright until it lists (some might say romantically) to one side like a great ship sinking, the water spilling the rubber seals, cracks, anyplace it can until a bubbling froth no one will ever see rises up and she's gone. All that in two minutes. There are those who have stopped on the narrow span, one of the longest suspension bridges in the world, braving the wind, to gaze down at the dark water. They wave and point, finding nothing in the surge and snow and night-dark except perhaps what they imagine to be a glint of fender, a fleck of what was but is now completely gone—rising out of the blinding wind and snow.

∴

That day she went down to the Lower Peninsula to visit X, who managed a food market in Traverse City. They went driving, two lovers alone. Now they're parked in his tan Chevy Nova at the end of Mission Point. See them? Her boyfriend has his pants shackling his ankles and she has her shirt above her shoulders. A beastly, dark night, raging gusts rock the car on its shocks. The words whispered aren't much different from the radio noise, vows floating over static, meant more to tickle the timpanic membrane than anything else—and gooseflesh on her arms proves to him that his breath in her ear is arousing, and the words she speaks, with her lips against his neck, don't come anywhere near his ears, but he feels them anyway, a soft, moist flutter of lips and tongue. It is the solitude and joy in this stuffy car in the center of the absolute rage of the elements that amuses, draws us to them, makes us wish there might be some way to pluck her out of the car, to warn her of her pending fate. Twenty yards down the sand, Lake Michigan churns wildly with the same violence that sends supertankers to their grave, and yet they are going at it, finding handholds, testing new courses with their fingers. The external rage of wind that will in a few hours send this girl's car off the bridge now helps them to feel that the only solace and relief and safety in this world lies in the intermingling of their bodies, while outside the earth breathes hellfire.

"Hey, I love you," he says. They are both getting dressed in the car. He has his legs bent and has to shift his hips from side to side to get his pants on. She is shutting the clasp of her bra. Now that they're done, it feels cold in the car.

∴

When she was waiting tables the summer before at one of the tourist hotels, he was bussing and washing dishes. When he saw her wiping the soap spots off the rim of a glass with the edge of a linen napkin, something in the nimble way she held the glass, her small, very white finger rolling the edge, caught his eye. He looked from those fingers to her arm, up the long, slender side, to her neck; she wasn't even facing him but was turned sideways toward the tall windows opening to the late evening light. That was how they did it, setting up for breakfast after the dinner shift. Out in the lobby the elderly clientele sat talking softly. Someone was heaving up the old staircase, making the wood steps cry. The hotel was like that, creaky and old. Helen Keller had stayed there, years ago, on a speaking tour. Next he saw the back of her hair, pinned up, dark black, whirling around to the base of her neck. And later, at the funeral, standing before the empty casket, he remembered that first summer. For X, at that time, it was an extremely simple thing to fall in love. "I know damn well I'm in love," he told a friend that night, smoking cigarettes at the end of the pier. It felt like a love of extreme depth, and it seemed mirrored by the long, shimmering breadth of unmoving water that opened up past Little Traverse Bay into the larger lake.

It was the way she held the glass; she was alone, the rest of the shift left an hour ago, and she stayed—he presumed—for the extra five bucks setup duty offered.

"Don't go," he says in the car. "I mean stay down here. What the hell. Your old man's not going to, well, I mean what's he going to do?"

She kisses his neck. "My father needs me back . . ." She speaks sadly, moving away from him, sits a second, and then begins to wiggle into her long green coat while he takes the side of his hand and, bending up, tries to swipe some of the frost off the inside of the windshield. All of the windows are covered with frost. He sweeps his side clean and leans across her lap to do hers. Then he climbs silently into the backseat and, using an old rag, circling it vigorously, makes portals in the back windows.

"I'm sorry, I didn't mean to bring it up," he says in a persuasive tone. The lies he told were usually small ones about his physical prowess (he said he could run a sub-five mile—he couldn't; said he could high-jump six feet—he couldn't).

"You did mean to bring it up." She sits straight up in her seat, works the rubber band into a loop, again putting both elbows up, and makes a ponytail. He reaches around and touches the hair at the back of her neck—remembering, or perhaps not remembering, that first view of her, at the hotel, last summer—and he feels a tightness in his legs.

"No, I didn't," he says. "No, wait, I'm not telling the truth. I did want to bring it up." He moves his hand away, putting both on the sides of the steering wheel. "I wanted to bring it up. Yes, I'm a little tired of your old man. I mean isn't it a crime being such a hard-ass . . . I mean, for God's sake you're legal now. You're not his."

He turns the key and feels soothed by the roar of the engine. He spent the whole day yesterday underneath the car, in his garage, with only a space heater going to keep warm. Grit from swabbing out the oil pan was still beneath his fingernails. He'd adjusted the timing with one of those old-fashioned spark gauges; he'd gone over the plugs with a clean rag.

The love he felt that first night, after speaking of it to his friend Mac, had gone on for months; they went out on very tentative dates—to the one movie theater in Petoskey, the Gaslight, where *Jaws II* was showing about a year after its

release. The love had stayed flat and firm and shimmering even
after those first visits to her father up in the Upper Peninsula.
Propped on large, gray cinder blocks, her father's house wasn't
much more than an elongated shack with a tin roof and a
muddy, dog-mauled front yard scattered with the usual assortment of junk: old car axles, a differential assembly, something
that was once probably a sheet of corrugated iron but now resembled a lace antimacassar of rust. Along the side was a
woodpile and a chopping stump with an axe lodged deep in its
side.

"You don't love me." She speaks with a flat nasal affect; it's
an unattractive voice, really, even to those who are used to it.

"I do love you." He eases the car back, does a reverse K turn.
Sand has blown along the edge of the parking lot. Signposts
shake in the wind. He snaps the heater on.

"My father is a good man," she says. "He worked his ass off
to support us, and you know that has to mean something."

"He hates my guts."

"He just doesn't want me down here overnight. He wants
to know where I am. And, well, the truth is he needs me . . ."

"So call him." He drives out into the main road. In the summer it is all fruit trees, farmhouses, wind-brushed fields of
golden weeds, and past those the brilliant blue of Lake
Michigan. Before his big brother Danny died in Vietnam they
used to come here to swim. He really was too young to remember, but he had a snapshot of it, one of those old ones
with the white border, and on the back, neatly stamped, beside the word Kodak, the date in red ink. In that photo his

52

brother stood in the sand, his face midsummer brown, in a tight white T-shirt. In the crook of one arm he held his little brother like a football.

He drives off the Point onto the wide, snow-swept main street of Traverse City. Color seems bled from the shop buildings on both sides, and there isn't much action going on except for two pickups parked across from a tavern. Dry, powdery snow sifts across the street.

"It's just—just that I know that this is the right time for you to stay overnight."

He's in love with the image of it; when he woke with her in his arms, there would be that pale blue light outside from the new snow; the soft silence of his room above the store, up close to the rafters. He'd make love to her again, then, but this time afterward they'd lie with that abandon, that wild hope, of two lovers who had slept through an entire night together for the first time. He hadn't slept with a girl a whole night through and still had that sense that the act was, by all means, a sacred one. In sleep there were secret movements and motions that one never knew. Pulling in front of the shop he feels a new urgency. He'll beg and plead.

He says, "I want you to stay. I want to, well, I feel like I have to beg you but I don't want to beg you. It's just that— well, I know he's going to be pissed off, and maybe you'd better stay down here for a few days, or I don't know, I mean why don't you move in with me? You can work in the shop. I need an extra hand. And for God's sake, this weather. You shouldn't be driving in this weather."

"No," she says. He kills the motor and in the silence that opens up there is the roar of the wind, coming from the west, pushing past the buildings—and the grainy white hiss of metal being blasted by dry snow.

∴

Was it the force of her father's personality, or something physical, that drove her away, back over the bridge? He never knew, exactly. Crossing the threshold of the house in the Upper Peninsula, he met a man wearing loose reading glasses, an old-fashioned ribbed undershirt, with hairy arms well defined from outdoor work. Her father did odd jobs, hauled lumber, chopped wood, pieced together a semblance of living from whatever that depressed region offered up. He spoke in a soft but firm voice that led one to believe he was from further north, maybe Canada. There was a hint of French floating around in his words.

"What do you do, son?" her father wondered. It came out as a prompt, fatherly question, with only a hint of that hardness he'd heard in other girlfriends' dads.

"I manage a food market, at Traverse City," he said.

A few seconds opened up after he gave an answer; the house was cold and drafty. It was late in the afternoon on a fall day. There was a football game, the Lions, with the sound down on the television set. "That's good. At least you have employment," he said, sipping his beer without tipping the can, just drawing the foam rising out of the hole.

"The Lions certainly stink."

"Yes, they do."

"They're worse this year, now that they're trying those new formations."

"Yeah."

They talked football a while longer and then they excused themselves and went out walking in the fresh air. The road skirted the state forest, most of it replanted pines in neat rows—rows deep and long and splicing through each other at angles, so that when he looked down them he got a strange infinite sense, a sense that there were Scotch pines stretching on into eternity, and yet ending directly before his eyes.

"My father's pretty quiet," she said. She meant something else but wasn't going to say it, he could tell. The smell of sap hung in the air. He was glad fall had arrived so quickly. The tourists had cleared out of town and his work at the market was slow and easy.

"You should come down and live with me," he said. It was the open span of road that prompted him to make the statement, the movement of their feet over the old concrete.

"I can't leave him right now," she said. "I can't really explain it, but he's not stable. I don't know what he'd do without me."

They walked up to the next entry road—dusty brown dirt ending at a chain-link fence that posted the state forest regulations on a white sign. "It's just that when my mother died, I kind of took over the role of . . ." That was as far as she was going to go. She took him by the neck and kissed him. "Come on. Let's do it here."

"Here?"

"Yeah, why not. No one comes down this way. They come in along the southern part. Even the rangers don't come up here."

So they made love, and later, after the funeral, the next summer, he'd remember that abrupt end to the conversation, the way she hung from his neck like a kid, the feeling of her body in her tight jeans, her legs firm, locked behind him, falling back into a blanket of pine needles and moss; it was cold that day and the places where their flesh touched seemed to burn with unnatural heat. He came quickly, was done with it, and the question he had raised on the road, of her coming down to live with him, was lost. But on the beach, alone on the spot where he imagined his brother had once held him under the crook of his arm, that moment in the woods seemed pivotal. The questions he might have asked, the digging he might have done if he hadn't allowed his search for the truth, for answers, to evaporate his lust, and his love, and the sensation of the sky being held up over their heads by the tips of pine trees. Love, he would later think, on the beach, is a dispelling of reality; it tears the truth out from under you.

The funeral, held at a parlor in Sault Ste. Marie, was the strange occasion you might expect because, of course, no body had been recovered. A simple pine casket had been selected and people were allowed to place into it things that represented her life in some way; there were ribbons that had held her hair back, small curls of yellow and blue, placed there by her aunt Grace; there was her maroon high school letter sweater, a big felt varsity K, for Kalkaska, with a silver set of wings she earned running cross-country one year; there were dolls she had once held and the Ovation guitar she had played, the rounded bottom tucked into the corner of the red silk lining. It looked a bit strange, somewhat like a body.

"What did you put in?" her father asked. He had lost weight and was gaunt around the chin where the flesh seemed stretched out. In a few months, he would die of lung cancer— two weeks of smothering, his left lung collapsing and his right barely able to process blood and oxygen.

"Nothing," he said. "I couldn't think of anything. What did you put in?"

"I put the guitar in, along with her mother's wedding ring and a few other such objects," he said softly, and then moved away, back to his spot next to the registration book, where he slowly smoked a cigarette.

∴

"Get your hands off me," she says, pushing him back against his side of the front seat. All he did, really, was nudge her a bit.

"What's the deal? I mean I don't fucking get this. All I'm asking is that you stay here for one night." He tries to regain his balance, to put aside the little shove with an explanation, but it's not enough—nor should it be, he thinks immediately.

"You hit me," she says, getting out.

"I didn't hit you."

"You shoved me."

"Look, it's just that I'm so frustrated. It's late. It's near what? Two? and you have three hours to drive when you could just call and make some excuse, the snow or something." He follows her to her little Japanese compact. The car has an inch of snow on top, which makes it look even smaller.

She's crying now, her key shaking in the lock, the snow cascading off the door and roof.

"You'd better clean that off," he says, but she's in the car, closing the door. Before she can lock it, he opens it and puts his body partway in. She seems remote and tiny in that dark little space, with only the frail brown-green light from the dash on her face; she ignites the engine, a frail putter of four cylinders that makes him wince, and then she turns the lights on—behind him the wind is increasing; the snow is thickening, blasting against his ears.

"I'm sorry," he says, holding his voice steady and calm. He has used the slightest force against her and she has responded in turn: there is something, he knows, in the formula, some acute sensitivity to his actions. He feels the answer; he knows the answer, but at that moment he is unable to find it. He's like the kid going to the board in class knowing how to solve the equation, chalk in his fingers, but too filled with panic to work it out.

"You fucking pushed me. It's as simple as that, really," she says again. The wipers are going, moving slowly, hardly able to remove the swaths of snow from the front.

"I'm sorry. I said I'm sorry. Really, I am. I just want you to stay here." He hunches down into the doorway of the car, his chin touching her thigh.

"I can't. Not now. Especially now."

He remembers her hand on that glass in the hotel dining room; he stands and watches her drive down the street; a salt spreader is coming the other way, rotating a yellow splay of light over her path and spewing rock salt. The roads are still clear. It's just the opening act of the first blizzard of the year. He waits for something, for a blink of brake lights, to let him know that she's thinking of him.

When the funeral was almost over he went back behind the building with Jim, an old high school friend of hers, who had a joint rolled and ready to go. They took a few sweet tokes, hiding in the snow behind a large maple, and then began to talk.

"Her old man was a strange one," Jim admitted, "and, yeah, there was some strange talk going around about her and him, but nothing that could be proved one way or another. Her mom had been horribly unhappy. There had been some trial separations and the like, so far as I can tell, but, still, talk is only talk, and I guess no one really knows."

∴

O n the beach the next summer he thinks of several factors, his toes dug down beneath the warmth to the cold of night that is still there. He might have used real force, taken her out of the car, dragged her up the stairs to his apartment and forced her to stay; maybe with force of that kind she would have given into him eventually—the erotic elements opening up somehow. They'd wake to the cold room, the soft muffle of a half foot of snow over the rafters. He'd get up and go downstairs to get the store open, leaving her a note or something—begging, just plain begging forgiveness. Or else, down on his knees, he might have found the right way to ask her to forgive him for that one, tiny nudge (and it was a small push, maybe even accidental). Maybe the right question posed would have opened up the thing with her father like a knife through ripe fruit, and then she might have told him about it. Then she would've gone up to his room and lain with him, spending the night. He would've listened tenderly. He would have opened his heart to her story. There would've been snow heavy overhead and, outside, once the winds finally died down, the deep silence that draws everything near. In the morning her car would've been down in the street, beneath a blanket of white, and he would've helped her clear it off, sweeping the windows clean with the brush, kicking it off the fenders, and he would've pushed from behind until she was out in the street, giving her one last heave until the tires caught the bare pavement and she was on her way, safe and sound, heading back up toward the Mackinaw Bridge, which by then would have been clear, dry, white with salt, arching gracefully over the straights.

A VISIT FROM JESUS

Jan worked at a market in the town of Traverse City, Michigan, known chiefly for its fine cherries and cherry products, and, once a year, a festival in that fruit's honor. For two months she'd been dating X, the market's owner. A hardworking middle-aged man, with fine blue eyes set into a thin face, he treated her at first, and even later, with a quaint formality. For weeks after their first kiss he seemed afraid to touch anywhere beyond her face. In the storage room they drank coffee together, sitting on top of unpacked corrugated boxes of canned goods. He fumbled with his words, wrung his hands in thought. His first wife had died years ago in a strange boating accident on Walloon Lake. He spoke of it only once and tears came to his eyes. He lived in a small apartment above a bakery, up a rickety flight of wooden stairs. They drank coffee there, too, sitting on the back steps, enjoying the night wind. They walked alone together at Mission Point. It was early fall. The tourists had cleared out for the winter. He didn't talk much, but it didn't seem to matter. She liked his silence. She held his hand and felt the wrinkles around his knuckles, the hard calluses around the pads of his fingers. When he did kiss her, she ran her hand around the back of his neck and tried to soothe him. It was like this for a month. Walks, drinking coffee, holding hands and kissing. Once, choking over his own words, he said: You're so beautiful, a young girl, only twenty-four, who, like an angel, has come into my life. And she was beautiful, with long golden-honey hair, and rich-fleshed lips, soft beyond anything, and wide brown eyes. That afternoon she held his face in her hands and bathed him in kisses, working down to the open collar of his shirt.

Business slowed at the store as it usually did in the off-season. She swept the floors and restocked items while he worked over his books and listened to the radio. She heard the faint clicking of the calculator keyboard. Occasionally, he stopped, looked up at her, and smiled.

For her part, she told him the basics. When she was seventeen she had married Bob Karr, her high school sweetheart. He went off to the Persian Gulf War and came back bitter and confused and, he claimed, extremely ill from desert fungi. All day he scratched himself. She kept the story simple, not wanting her past to cloud things with this soft, quiet man, but she implied that her first husband, on his return from the war, had changed. He was abusive, she said. She moved back in with her parents in Paw Paw, attended a nearby community college for two years. Then, one summer afternoon, Bob shot himself. Shortly thereafter, as if in response to this tragedy, both her parents were killed in a car accident. And so she moved north to Traverse City and found her job working at the market with X.

All went well, deep into the heart of the Michigan winter. They made love on December 3, in his apartment, on clean, starch-smelling sheets. She went home to her apartment, which was upstairs from a small tavern, and said her absolutions and prayers—for in her own private quarters, alone, she was devout, bending down, her arms folded on the soft poplin bedspread. While she was thus prone she heard a small, shivery, choking voice coming through the wall over the din of the tavern below. It was Christ speaking. He called her. She floated up to heaven and he was there, seated in an armchair. His looks were plain. His nose was that of a boxer's, broken at least once, with a small shift of cartilage. She tried not to stare. His eyes were agate-colored. His skin sallow. He had a slight lisp. On his head the crown of thorns dug into a mop of yellow-blue hair, as fine as silk, cut in a bowl cut. He spoke carefully, to frame his thoughts.

"My dear," he began. "This man you're seeing. This one X," he said. "I must discuss this case with you."

"Yes, my Lord," she said, looking directly into his eyes.

"I have brought you here to protect you. To grant you my grace. To provide you with, well, ah, with some information."

"Yes," was all she could say. She hadn't expected him to be

so human, so natural. He reached up to wipe his nose, caught himself.

"There is darkness there in front of your eyes, and before you witness violence, are violated, I wished to bring it to, ah, to your attention. In his trunk, his footlocker, whatever it's called, you should look. Take great care. It will come to you. And then you must return to me and we'll discuss our—how should I say it?—next course of action."

He dropped her back to earth, her fall softened by the cheap boardinghouse mattress. The roar from the tavern, the thump of a bass line from an old Eagles song ("Hotel California"), rose from below along with that chalky aftermath of a hundred burning cigarettes and the occasional hard click of pool balls being broken apart.

The next afternoon she stole the extra key to his apartment from the hook behind the door in the storage room. Her lover was meeting with a canned goods supplier and was out front, clipboard in hand, checking stock when she left under the pretense of needing to go to the drugstore for something personal. His apartment was stuffy with steam heat. The afternoon sun burned through the windows. The footlocker, painted military green with his name stenciled along the side in white block letters, was already open and she saw them immediately, magazines unfolded. Young boys with older men, legs splayed wide open, mouths agape with what amounted to pain, violation, screams that met the afternoon silently but rose in her ears and in the afternoon dust floating up into the sunlight. One boy was gagged. Another had his hands tied behind his back. Oh, oh, she said, falling to her weak knees. The isolation of this part of Michigan took hold of her. She felt everything that X had filled up, all that solitude, the loss of her parents, her soul, empty out again. Her bowels shifted. She clawed her hair in grief. She didn't go back to the store but walked to her room and lay down. Downstairs it was silent, an afternoon at the bar, only a couple of drifters sipping beers, watching the smoke rise from their cigarettes. She lay for a long time. The phone rang in the front room and her answering machine came on, clicked, beeped, and she heard X's voice—soft-spoken, concerned. The phone rang again—she rose out of sleep to listen; the machine beeped and the voice that came over it, shivery-cold, bloated, was the voice of the devil. She recognized it immediately. It twirled around the tongue. It hissed. It was static and energy discharge. It was the wind off Lake Michigan at two a.m.

That night, at the store, she killed X with a box cutter, lodged it first directly into his windpipe, driving down and then to the side, gutting him the way her father used to gut deer, calmly. He was found in the storage room, with his head propped gently onto a bag of presifted flour, his legs open and his pants off. And of course the police suspected her first, and after talking to a few locals, they began their hunt; but she had vaporized, risen up into the state, gone into the woods in one way or another to hide.

She was in a hotel in Houghton, way up, looking out over Lake Superior, which with the howling wind was chrome blue at midday; she was on her knees at her bed praying for forgiveness when she was, again, called up to Christ; he was there this time in a plaid shirt with a bad cold, trying not to sniff, a box of tissues on his knees.

"You didn't listen to me," he said. She was surprised at his brisk, businesslike tone. "I told you to come to me, to talk with me before you made your next move."

"I didn't have time," she said, looking into his eyes. His hair had grown a bit and he had to shake his head to get it out of his face.

"Ah, that's the way with the world," he said. "Nobody wants to come back to me, to talk it over. It's act first. Discuss later."

"I'm sorry," she said.

"It's this weather." He spoke as if to someone else, out into the void behind her. "It's driving everybody nuts. I mean even I have cabin fever."

"So I'm forgiven?"

"Well, I'll look into it. I mean I'll think about it."

Again her fall was eased by a cheap mattress. She lay on the bed listening for police sirens and heard only the cold rasp of wind off the lake. Guys in the room next door were drinking beer, laughing, banging around. She fell asleep and awoke the next day to the sizzling sound of the devil's voice coming beneath the door with the wind.

"If he has to think about it, you'll have to come with me," he said.

"Oh." She blinked, sat up, drew her arms across her breasts.

"I mean who has time?"

"I guess I don't," she said, but she wasn't sure.

∴

One sees the likes of her everywhere; disposed of, fucked, torn and battered. Let's be frank, for once. She didn't end up going with the wind-voiced devil, or with Christ, who, taking his own good time, decided eventually to grant her a stay of forgiveness; she was found dead by the hotel maid, crumpled with her legs up against her stomach in a small blue robe; she had a garter belt on, and a small teddy the man from the room next door demanded she wear, and then the other guy who joined him later, coming over when he heard things getting hot and heavy; her skin was as pale as the sky over the lake that morning, and she had shoot marks up and down her arms from two hard years of high-grade smack; there were signs of abrasion in her vagina, which the medical examiner attributed to rape. The good doctor, shining his penlight into her eyes to check her pupils, made note of beauty—ice white and blue mixed in the dead nonmovement of her eyes; he thought of his fifteen-year-old daughter who still gave him hugs and seemed protected by his love, but he wasn't a stupid man, and he knew the world, this world, this great country of his, could eat anything, absolutely anything, up.

PETROUCHKA
[WITH OMISSIONS]

A pianist was beset with panic because his right hand
had frozen up, grown heavy, during a Schubert sonata, missing several notes during the Andante, sending a soft murmur—accompanied by hard biting coughs from angry
throats—through the audience. All was suddenly asunder, his
command faltering, the normal alliance between his skill, his
talent, and what might be called genius, broken. The audience
settled into a stunned silence, an aural black hole from which
emerged a few more tight coughs. As most everyone already
knows, his grand celebration, his triumphant return from
Moscow, was ruined. And as many of you might have guessed,
the sense of panic that began that night would not subside. His
fingers—in the parlance of his profession—stayed heavy.
Those fingers—I'll admit—are mine.

∴

The bridges spanning the Cuyahoga were rusted up, some down, others sadly in *medias res*, either lowering for a train or rising gallantly for an approaching slag barge. To re-live old times, I was riding the Rapid into the city, praying for my father, who was in the hospital; praying or trying to find a way into prayer but not exactly sure if I believed in anything aside from what I felt when I was playing Bach. But I mouthed something: God grant my father (certainly you know him, probably have listened to him play when he was principal French horn with the Philharmonic), grant him whatever it is you grant, give him his place in heaven; allow him to pursue some eternal music, and then I opened my eyes to take in the sight of the train car, smeared with grime, fingerprinted win-ter mud on the walls, the seats orange and beige plastic. When I got to the hospital I half expected to find my father in his bed buzzing his mouthpiece, or his fingers twitching through a complex bit of fingering. Instead, I found a man who had just been given his second shot of morphine, more than he needed for pain, a dose to help him over to the other side. He spoke in the light, airy voice of someone stoned: Like I've said, son, you're playing too wide, son, he said, for God's sake you're playing too wide, you should stick with one or two composers, linger on them, explore a terrain and master it, be-come, you know, like one of those arctic explorers who spend years just trying to get to one place and back alive.

∴

[O]mitted from this section: He disagreed with his father. Of course there in the hospital room he wasn't
about to argue. To linger over one or two composers for an entire career seemed like an exercise bordering on cultist adoration, maybe religion; he was no monk. Later that night his
father died. Nothing dramatic. Then days of arrangements—
the funeral parlor, the minister, and then the funeral, attended
by a few retired members of the Cleveland Philharmonic.
When he got back to New York he met up with Antoinette
right away, at a place on Madison near her building. When
someone tells you something just before he dies, he said, it
kind of sticks to you like a residue—is that the word?—and
you can't, at least I can't, just shrug it off. And she turned to
look up at him, over her spoon, with wide gray eyes, considering what he'd just said; but her eyes were off slightly, drifting away when she tried to focus. Before lunch she'd gone into
the bathroom and snorted something (cocaine? heroin?) from
a square of brown wrapping paper. He was a beautiful man
with great talents and fine clothing. He was a man who would
take her away to some domestic place, she thought. He, in turn,
felt the deep shame that came from laying out the particulars
of his private life to a woman who was, clearly, under the influence of medication. (At that point he was only partly aware
of her addictions and thought it was something she was taking
for pain in her ankle.) In the end he'd leave the restaurant and

71

go out into one of those astonishingly clear days, bright cold weather, just before Christmas when the whole metropolis, at least the Upper East Side, seemed to establish itself as a center for high-class gift giving. In a few weeks, up in those apartments overlooking Central Park, women would unwrap mink stoles from great long boxes; men would be led blindfolded to the bowels of parking garages to see, unveiled from beneath clean canvas tarps, their new sedans.]

∴

You hear about this stuff: a pianist from Mexico—most talented guy in the whole country, a big national figure, an asset to his country, a cultural ambassador by virtue of his abilities—who just folded up halfway through a sonata (take your pick: Beethoven, Brahms, whatever), stopped playing, slammed down the cover, stomped off the stage, and never ever again touched a keyboard of any kind. A young opera star from Verona who damaged her vocal cords in a screaming match with her husband and never sang again. The year of my first European tour we were in Italy for a break, running along the beach, tossing a Frisbee, working up a nice rhythm—husband to wife, wife to husband, the passing of the disk—and I was going to try one fancy catch even though we were going for a record number of passes, counting each one, and I was trying to catch it backhanded, racing to the side to meet Margaret's smooth, flat toss heading directly toward my outstretched arm, my hand, my fingers—clawed open in anticipation—a bit tight because I'd been working all morning, trying to meet the technical demands of a Liszt piece. (For his part, Liszt was swallowed up by his virtuosity.) But then my foot hit a rock—the only rock on the whole half-mile stretch of beachfront—and I found myself balled up, fetal, with a toenail snapped down the middle and a broken toe. With my weight on Margaret's shoulders, we followed the goat path up to the apartment. The next morning, if I remember correctly, and I think I do, I kept my sore foot off and played everything *sans pedale*, pecking through Chopin's Sonata in B Minor, pounding the Scherzo— which as you probably know means joke in Italian—feeling suddenly light, airy, and purged of all deficiencies. Without the pedal the famous bass line was submerged, and the piece was restored to a flat empty world that Chopin never wanted; a stripped, destroyed, bare-boned perfection. I'd meet Antoinette at a reception a few weeks later—along with the other well-wishers—handing me, as so many did at that time, a large bundle of roses, still dripping, wet, and fresh.

∴

About a year after my fingers got heavy, we rented an estate up the Hudson, a place to recuperate, to gather new energies, to mend. At Juilliard I was teaching technique, placing my fingers on top of fingers, putting students through the rigors of my methods: one of the last of the believers in tapping exercises, one magazine called me. The same method gave Glenn Gould his fine, pointed sound. The fingers of one hand were placed over those of the other, forcing the fingers to become acquainted with the notes, to learn them physically. At the house I set up a Steinway beneath the windows of the so-larium. I'm going to torture the fucking thing the way it tor-tures me, I used to say to Margaret. In a few weeks the instrument began to produce a tinny, off-tune bar-piano sound, as if waxed paper were lodged under the hammers. I couldn't play without thinking of dusty Wild West towns, of those parlor uprights abandoned to the husk-dry afternoons of the Central Plains.

One afternoon, Jake the tuner came in for his scheduled visit, arriving with his old duct-taped valise and his droopy jeans, and we had a conversation that went something like this:

Man, this is a horrible thing you're doing to this piano, Martin, just horrible. You've got to at least get a dehumidifier in this place and clear out those ferns and maybe block off a few of the windows.

Really, Jake, I guess you feel some deep personal need to humanize pianos. I suppose it's part of your job—the way some people humanize, say, dogs.

Well, yeah, I take care of them and tune them, and each one has a kind of personality, sure. Yeah, I guess I do human-ize, if that's the word, although I think the word you want is personify.

A bundle of wires and felt and wood, a fat cast-iron frame and a soundboard, really, nothing, nothing. It's a sickness to say it's anything else except those things, Jake, for Christ sake. It's a sickness to think the way you think—even if it's your job. It's nothing, nothing, nothing in the world at all, nothing, so if I want to let the thing rot in the heat, then so be it. Now if you don't mind I'd like you to get out of here.

∴

[Omitted in this section: the long conversations with Irene on the patio, gin in hand, as they watched the flat stone barges being tugged toward New York. Left out are those resolutions made under great duress, the vows, the statements of fact, the cold/hot touches, the intense sessions with the shrink, the feelings expressed and reexpressed, the intense vibration he felt along his palm, the physical therapy sessions, the hot wax treatments, the arthritis specialists, the acupuncturists. (Omitted from this section of omissions: he couldn't stand the tinny sound the damaged Steinway made, but he went ahead and lived with the hope that his abuse of the piano would somehow eliminate the weight in his hands, as if his fingers might, in the hope of making clear sharp notes out of the bar room sound, press firmly, resolutely upon each note.)]

∴

The carnality of it, the brute squeezing, the concave twitch of thigh muscles when you're pushing hard, deep into the center, that terminus. Then the lifting sensation, peeling back, the void, the sense that some feckless bit of life has slipped away, lost. (Just as when working over a piece I might make a slight trill, a grace note, finished before my awareness of it set in.) It was *to be done*—and it would be labeled perfect and brilliant, coming from a place hidden deep within the work itself, and so it was when I was with her, her Italian stockings twisting in a helix along the top of a chair. Outside in the blue winter night, cars pushed through the slush on Park Avenue. Down the street the museum was closed for the night, the great display cases, the paintings, shrouded in darkness, the coat racks empty. Behind the museum a blanket of white covered Central Park. Trees eased under the weight of fresh snow. Alone in my orgasm I'd begun thinking about how in a few days I might take Margaret and Sylvia—at that time Sylvia was about eight—shopping on Fifth Avenue, where, spread out on sheets of damp cardboard in front of Tiffany's, vendors in rags would plead with us, rubbing their hands together, stamping their feet to stay warm, selling cheap imitation cashmere scarves.

∴

[Omitted here is the perplexity he felt over his split feelings, the dualism he felt taking Sylvia shopping on Fifth, slipping her little hand into his glove so he could warm it up; hiking across the park, slapping snow in each other's faces. He loved fresh snow on Central Park but despised the way, a few short hours into the morning, the snow was defiled by ski tracks, sled marks, people jogging, the frenetic urgency with which New Yorkers threw themselves into exercise.]

∴

Eventually I gave up trying to get rid of the weight in my fingers.

∴

[Omitted in this section: A few days after returning from Russia, in a practice room at Carnegie Hall, he'd sat plucking the keys, listening to the deadened sound of notes absorbed by the acoustic tiles; he ran through the nocturnes; he'd played flawlessly, relaxing the tops of his hands, rolling across the notes (as his first teacher used to describe it, creating a fluid movement into the notes, through them, a rolling motion), pointing each one but not too carefully. You don't want to make the listener aware of the notes, one of his teachers used to say. You want to seduce the listener into thinking he's actually *hearing* notes, when in truth he's hearing Chopin, only Chopin. The old battered practice piano—soft from years of pounding—produced a dog-eared tone, slightly yellow. He finished, exhausted, and rested his brow against the board; then he got up, stretched out his legs, and opened the door. It was like unsealing a vault, allowing wonderful sound to flow out and escape into the stale hallway. From down the hall came the sandy shuffle of ballet slippers across floorboards. (This was a sound he loved from early memories of music school and summer music camp in the Midwest.) Antoinette appeared a moment later, standing for a second in the doorway, holding her coat tight at the collar, shivering. Her face was narrow but thoughtful and led up to blond hair so fine it eluded control; it sprang from clips, slid out from the tightest band, flew from any hat. He saw that her eyes had given over to some fear. Her stare had a subdued gloss. She blinked rapidly. Her ankle was bad. She'd fallen during a leap—something called a grand Jeté—arriving back to the stage slightly off balance, misaligning her foot so it received the brunt of the force. An understudy had taken her place. She was alone with her injury. None of the company had visited her dressing room. They feared being jinxed. Ice was applied in bright blue packs. An X-ray revealed a stress fracture, but there was something more. A tendon was pulled. I'm fucked, she said, because Francisco has decided to sideline me. Bending down, she rubbed her ankle softly and then, forming a ring with both hands, twisted her hands as if trying to remove a lid from a jar. The doctor had given her an injection of cortisone. She stood back up, put her heels together, gathered her hands, raised them above her head, opened them apart, formed an arch, and lifted up onto the tops of her flattened toes. He felt completely the beauty and sickness of this abnormal position; even after years of watching ballerinas find this position, it still hurt to see; it was odd. Against the nature of feet and bones and even the heart itself.]

∴

We're in bed. That's where our wings were attached, you know, she's saying. I think of angel wings plucked clean off by the hand of Christ. Under the sheets her bad ankle rests against mine and, to be honest, our legs are entwined and I'm reeling from the incredible way I played a nocturne during practice, the manner in which it came out of me but also the nocturne itself—the solemn perfection with which the notes arrived. She twitches slightly. The luminous throb of Stravinsky's *Petrouchka* emerges from her stereo so softly we can hardly hear it. But when her cues come on she involuntarily gives a slight lift of one leg over another and her toes extend and she winces at the pain. The music has urged her to twitch. Like a rubber mallet tapping a knee. At dinner parties, sometimes even shopping, she'll hear a cue and in response, purely involuntary, she'll point a toe or swing a leg upward. I know the feeling. When I'm listening to a piece I've committed to memory my own fingers twitch, opening up the ghostly possibility of an unseen hand.

∴

[Omitted from this section: At his friend Bernard's suggestion he had read a story by Isaac Babel called "The Sin of Jesus," in which a sluttish hotel servant is given an angel by God, an angel she immediately smothers. Also omitted is the fact that he didn't know (really, he didn't) that he was going to spurn her after this last fuck; he hadn't the slightest idea that the chain of events would soon nullify his desire for Antoinette, which was based, in any case, mainly on rudimentary physical factors, which in themselves were coming out of his own good fortunes as a pianist. His career was ascendant while the affair was going. When his touch went, his desire went, too.]

∴

The light itself had a stony commitment to the land, spreading along the coastline as we arrived. Sylvia was out on the deck, leaning against the rail, letting the wind twist her hair. Great wondrous auburn hair flared by windblown sea spray. Her hips have grown, her legs lengthened, and she is no longer my little girl but something else, a woman at age sixteen leaning forward to examine the sea and approaching shoreline, a ballerina; she has studied ballet, learned its intricacies, graduated to dancing on pointe, and is in a small youth company in the city. I've tried to warn her away from the art form as a profession. But when I drop her off at the train in Tarrytown, I see in the way she hefts the bright blue tote bag, firmly up against her hip, that she's preparing herself to haul her gear across the concourses of airports. She has that rugged lackadaisical motion of an artistic drifter. Our trip to Nova Scotia is a way to get away from all of that. I'll have a long talk, maybe get her to see the light.

∴

[Omitted from this section: a huge slice of narrative time. He has left out just about everything. Years have passed. Deep struggles with himself, Margaret, art. He has resigned himself to teaching. Giving it his all. The day-in, day-out trials of fatherhood.]

∴

A couple of weeks after the fiasco at the Alice Tully Hall recital I was in the studio trying to record Bach's French

Suite (BMV 772), still pretty certain that the heavy-finger event during the concert was a fluke, jangled nerves, a momentary loss of resolve. Manager Man, as I call him, stood in the control room with the score in his hands, tracing a finger along the notes. At the Andante part—simple fugue motion from side to side, a rocking (when played correctly) between the two voices, not all that hard on the technical front but demanding exactness on the interplay of voices—in that softness I faltered and landed too hard on an E-flat, counteracting with a contrary voicing. Manager Man stared pensively through the plastic window; he had one of those piratic faces—augmented by his thick beard—with the expression of a man demanding a bounty. Let's call it a day, he crackled over the microphone. We'll do another take tomorrow, fresh in the morning. The next day New York was draped in a wintery mess. Snow fell down in clumps and melted into the sidewalks. The studio was near the Port Authority, along Forty-second Street, and from the sidewalk you could watch as buses arrived from the suburbs, emerged out of the Lincoln Tunnel, heaved up the looping concrete entrance ramps. This was a preposterously ugly and noisy neighborhood, especially when compared to the padded silence of the studio. For a long time I stood watching the action, unable to go inside. I could see it all. My recording career would draw to a silent close. My face—strangely round and young, an old publicity photo—would appear one last time on the cover of *Gramophone*; a ghostly CD would be released with embarrassing fanfare, bringing together scavenged pieces recorded in the previous years when precision and élan arrived from my

fingertips. Publicly, I'd remain silent about my inability to finish the French Suites. But of course rumors would seep out: his
abilities are gone; he's fucked up; he's taking drugs; he was
having an affair with that what's-her-name, that anorexic ballerina junkie, and it did something to him; he has a weird stage
fright thing going. In order to counter these rumors I'd say
things I believed to be true: that the recording process itself was
suspect; that notes should not be held hostage to material sur-
faces: the ferrous oxide of tape or the vestige of bits and bytes.
Nothing deserves to be locked into the singular silence of repetitive play. I'd make the grand claim (because that is what failing artists are best at, being grand) that notes should be held in
the lingering solitude of notations on the staff, not released into
the air, where they only dissolve and become nothing.

∴

[Omitted from this part: the fact that his manager, Bob
Falco, had an addiction to painkillers; that Bob had
once propositioned Antoinette, stating that he was in love with
her, saying it frankly, without mincing words, with devout
clarity: I love you. I can't help myself. I love you more than
life. There had been between them a zesty kind of erotic
charge that couldn't be denied; they were standing beneath the
artificial stars of Grand Central Station. No, no, you don't, she
said, turning, fleeing across the wide concourse, merging into
the swish footfalls, swinging valises, clutched pocketbooks.]

∴

A serrated kitchen bread knife, nothing special, at least when she was holding it between her fingers and slicing a loaf of baguette from Zabar's. The view from the window behind her, over the sink, opened across a barren, wintry Central Park. Gazing out on a clear day, I could just about see Antoinette's apartment on the other side, the window glass winking knowingly in the sunlight. Margaret was holding the knife and slicing down into the bread while I was talking about my preparatory schedule for the Alice Tully Hall concert. (Margaret advised me on how to schedule practice.) In a few days my concert career would be over. Between us was that steady but settled electric current produced by two adults trying to act normal for the sake of a child; we'd been at it for a week now, and something was cracking.

I found the note, she said softly. I found the note.

You what?

I found this.

Antoinette had that careful prep school script with elaborate, ornate swirls, the kind I associate with the education she received at whatever finishing school she went to in the Swiss Alps. I'd kept this one because in it she had reached a kind of passionate, sexy, poetic groove, an irresistible schoolgirl wildness. That's how I'd explain it to my friend Bernard, the principal cello for the Philharmonic, who in turn would tell me about the Hebrew word *pag'a*, which means (I think) two material bodies, as in the blade/flesh, meeting, deeply. I stood in the kitchen doorway while she cut down into the bread, that kind with the wonderfully ungiving crust that made chewing seem like good, intense work. She cut through the bread and deep between her index finger and thumb, the web of skin there. Then she rocked back on her heels and put her hand up into the air and let the blood drip down around her arm. Behind us, at the dining room table, Sylvia was singing to herself, drawing something, unaware. The meeting of two material bodies or agencies, Bernard was saying. We were drinking martinis at the Harvard Club on a rainy afternoon.

One can't help but think of Goliath's huge sword, of pocketknives, of razor blades—I think there's always a certain preordained aspect to getting cut by a blade, either accidentally or on purpose, as if that blade, and that blade alone, were meant to meet your skin, he said. But then again I might be talking out of my ass, he added.

I think you are, I told him. I think you're talking directly out of your ass.

Bernard chuckled resonantly. (Often cello players have voices that seem contrived to match their instruments.)

I said something like: Bernard, it's not that I actually felt the same pain she felt, of course, but I'm certain that I not only felt the same amount of pain, I'm sure I was feeling more pain. More than she was. Maybe it was a different kind of pain. My own. In a different way. But more of it.

You're a selfish prick, he said.

Then Sylvia came into the kitchen and saw us on the floor (My voice began shaking and I thought I might weep right there at the Harvard Club), and she started crying, too—you know, that raw kind of clinched-up pain of an eight-year-old;

you know, the pain kids feel on the keenest level. They know pain a hell of a lot better than we do. They respect the stuff. Know it firsthand. I swear she understood exactly what was going on and was grieving for both of us.

∴

[O mitted from this section: He wrapped the towel tight around Margaret's hand, told her to hold it, to stanch the flow, as he guided her out the service entrance to wait for the elevator. He despised Bernard, who seemed to think that knowing about religion, facts, slogans, sayings, proverbs, ancient questions from the Talmud somehow counted as living a solid life of belief. Bernard had conducted his own affairs, including one with a whip-thin girl named Andrea who couldn't have been more than sixteen, which had ultimately led to his divorce; his kids were out in Santa Cruz with his second wife. Also omitted from this section: Just after Margaret cut her hand and he was leading her through the lobby, asking the doorman to please hail a cab, he felt for the first time beneath the base of his fingers, radiating out from the center of his palm, a cold electric tingle that would, in later months, establish itself as one of the physical aspects of his failure.]

∴

[O mitted from this section: He used Antoinette as an example, saying, Do you remember that old friend of mine, from back when, from when you were just a little kid, that friend Antoinette, who fell, hurt her ankle, and then

couldn't dance? Do you remember her? Really? Good, because
she's just one good example of what can happen, and I know
I'm being, well, fatherly, but I have to say it, I really do, she
fell, just warming up was all, and she tore a ligament or something—I can't even remember the details—and her career was
over and she, well, she gave into it. She just couldn't go on.
Well, that's kind of off the subject and I don't mean to scare
you, and I know that you're not going to change your mind,
nor should you, sweetie, not at all, don't change your mind on
account of anything I say to you. I don't expect that at all,
would even be scared if you did change your mind, but it's important that you know that a career can become so unhinged
by such a little thing. I love you dearly, more than the world,
more than the earth itself; you and your mom, you two. Yes.
Yes, more than music itself, of course, that's easy to say. More
than music, much, much more.]

∴

[Omitted: A few years later he was walking through the
dunes, following the little paths worn into the poison
ivy and reindeer moss, looking out at the Atlantic, cool and
gray below a veldt of thick clouds; there were storms in the
air, a distant low grumble of thunder working in from the
east; so many years had passed and he still felt some ancient
grief prodding. He walked down to the dune head and stood
at the top and saw, down below, a man walking his dog, the
dog darting far ahead of him, reaching some compromise between his desire to run forever and his gratitude toward his

master before he stopped, looked back, and made a loop partway to the man and then forward again, so that along the
beach there was a pattern, a looping crochet of his paw prints;
and seeing this he wondered what kind of dog was best at
spotting, at working outward in concentric circles until the
thing thrown, or tossed, was found; dictated beneath the surface of the dog's mind were governing forces that led him to
do so, just as bees danced to give their fellows a message. Here
he was, alone on yet another morning, his fingers fine, having
practiced for two hours before dawn, softly so as not to wake
Margaret, who slept deeply and was never bothered by his
playing anyhow. He felt the grace. He knew it was there in the
notes, and he played, he was sure, without an error, a whole
cycle of Shostakovich etudes, beautiful pieces that reminded
him of Bach. This is the morning I get my touch back, he
thought, not sure if he would or not. But he did. He played a
bit of the Bach suite that had failed him years ago in the
recording studio; this time it came out fluid and beautiful. He
was saved. He woke Margaret up, ruffled her long hair, which
was just starting to turn gray, and buried his nose in it, lying
beside her, nudging against her legs until she yielded to him
and then, rolling over, waking, became alive with motion. I'm
going out, he said afterward, and he went down the flagstone
path wet with salt spray and dew and mounted the hill up to
the dunes and then the paths and now was watching the dog.
In this manner the touch would stop eluding him; he would
play again, first a recital at Juilliard for faculty, and after that
some larger venues until he was invited to Israel to play; he

would be greeted again with shouts of joy and flowers tossed onto the stage. He would never exactly know, of course, what had caused the long period of inability. All he could remember of Antoinette was the way her hair whirled around her ears and the tapping she made on his back when she came, her index finger working his spine like a Morse code key. In the fall of the next year he would return to the house and walk up this same dune at about the same place and stand at the same spot and look bewildered and bemused at the churning sea; on the sand that morning there would be someone walking, too, and that person would look up at him as if at an old friend and wave; she'd have a scarf tied up around her head, bright red, and a long, pale face (from what he could see) that gave off a sense of resolute survival—a cancer survivor, a self-starver. He'd go down to the beach to see what she looked like up close, and she would, surprisingly, prove to be an old student of his, a woman named Hillary who had given up trying to play professionally. She'd been sick, yes, but was recovering, according to her doctors, with miraculous zeal. She had a wonderful daughter who also played. And he would share with her the news of his daughter's success, her recent performance of *Petrouchka*. You look happy, she would say. I am. I am, he'd answer, looking out at the waves that seemed to approach somewhat reluctantly before looming over themselves, tearing headlong with great urgency into a marly white edge that was forming, reforming, and always pulling back.]

[ELYRIA MAN]

1

Thompson scrapes off the residual mud, the encrustation of years, with the blade of the shovel, with the edge of a crowbar from his truck, working carefully around my head, avoiding eyes and orifices until ultimately a face is revealed. He gives a soft exclamatory murmur. He's reluctant to uncover my eyes. He fears sockets. But he does it. The uncovering of eyes is a one-shot trick, not to be repeated. And in any case he has already quickly adapted to the ugliness of my features. He appreciates my originality, the leathery incarnation of a primal self, as he pauses, leaning on his implement, his hoe or his pitchfork (preferably the three-pronged variety). In the late-morning light I appear forsaken in my clench-jawed agony, my pale crumpled eye sockets, and my positioning in the earth:

one arm tossed back in a relaxed sleeping position. Think of those time-lapse films of couples sleeping together, making unconscious bodily adjustments, both working in what seems to be a congruence, eerily responding in turn to the other on the white wrinkles of fresh sheets.

In the silence of an Ohio field—the irrigation pipes dripping softly behind him—I look fetal, protean, like a newborn foal just before he ungathers his legs to stand for the first time. In the contours of my face is the ungainly intelligence of the greasy womb-wet newborn. Thompson stares down at my form rising up out of the earth and absently chews his tobacco, spits sideways, sniffs, coughs, unfolds the squares of his handkerchief and deposits phlegm, and then refolds it and carefully puts it into his coat pocket. The forsaken are nothing new to him. He's seen the look a hundred times at cattle auctions. In his wife's eyes. In the eyes of his kids.

2

Thompson was taking a soil sample when the blade of his shovel touched something firm. Often a digger unknowingly amputates an arm with the shovel blade, decapitates, disembowels the dusty nothingness from a puckered gut. It happens most of the time. The haphazard surgery of the blind digger: the blade driven under the force of a boot, applied pressure condensed to the edge. But Thompson was a careful man. When he felt something in the ground he paused to think about it, to consider his options.

3

In town that afternoon the Amish man named John, hitching his buggy to a post, is receptive to hearing about me. He's always wondered about bog folk. Ohio bog folk especially, he adds, looking down at the hard-baked street. Bouquets of Queen Anne's lace sprout from the cracks. The road is absurdly wide, as if speaking to some long-ago hope for greater commerce.

Me own father found one once down to Wooster, John the Amish says, and this one had a small noose-like apparatus around his neck and was gripping a sacred heathen ornament. Them bog people were idolaters of the most basic sort. Certainly they weren't God-fearing folk. No sir. They mocked the Lord. But nonetheless, I'd be interested to see your bog man.

Yes, do come down to the farm, Thompson says, cutting him short. He has limited tolerance for the seriousness of these men; they seem consumed with the chore of faith. He shakes John's meaty hand. The horse—a beautiful brown and white marbled roan—clomps the pavement. The Amish men shuffle into the tobacco shop (Thompson with them), peruse the racks of girlie magazines, sneak them into the safe confines of pastoral titles: *Farmlife. Horticultural Digest. Organic Farmer. Model Railroader.* There is comfort in eyeing the gaping lipped pinkness that (I figure) somehow reminds them of farmwork. Thompson carries the story of me with him into the sweet tobacco smell, orders a pouch of Captain Black Gold, watches as the girl named Irene moves about behind the counter. She's a high school dropout in bib overalls. Her breasts lie behind the right angles of taut denim. He loves the way the straps, secure in the metal hook–button contraption, put forth an illusion of restraint and looseness at the same time. In those overalls, her body never fails to remind him of the horse-harness physics that governs the use of John's buggy parked just up the street. The strange conspiratorial relationship between the horse—blinded on both sides by small rectangles of black—and the owner's whip. Taking the tobacco pouch into his hands, he squeezes to test its moisture; a soft spongy feel indicates a good seal, soft sugary strands ready to be lodged in his pipe. He loves the sensation of his thumb entering the bowl—creosoted and sticky—and packing it soft, lovingly, intuitively not too firm or too loose—the same way he had stuck his fingers into Irene. She smiles uncomfortably and tries to conjure me up. Never heard of bog people, she says. He mentions others—Scotland, the peat there. The best she can do is imagine a decomposed corpse, something from a horror movie, arms and legs akimbo, skin peeling in raglike sheets from his body. If I had my way (and I do, sometimes), she'd visualize one of Matisse's bronze sculptures, from the Jeanette series, a fine abstraction indicating both my primal elements—the stately elegance of my form—combined with the modern thrown-back motion of my arms, the movement into space, a diver launching cleanly into a universe of blue and white.

4

I'll come to be known as the Elyria Man, uncovered several miles to the south of that city, just as the Grauballe (original name: Hans) became the Grauballe Man. If you have to be named for a geographic region, this one is as fine as any, boring and nondescript in what most agree is the most mundane and utilitarian of states, a state that openheartedly loves blandness. (On hearing this, Ohioans gather themselves into a defensive hunch.) Thompson embraced Ohio. He embraced John Glenn as the state hero. What more starkly boring symbol than a man circling the earth in a capsule equipped with outmoded gear, leather strapping, already ancient at launch time, spinning in the silence of space only to plunge back and sponge upon that act for the rest of his life? Thompson and I both agree that it would be better to remain up there, to be slung by gravity's twirl out into the void until radio contact faded out. Or better to return to earth, heat shield failing, in a blooming orchid of raw flame and burning metal, striking the Atlantic landing zone in a geyser of steam.

5

Ramrod straight, my great-uncle Stan was himself a bog man— the Minnesota variety discovered just north of Red Lake in that wondrous result of paludification. Ramrod Man was grimfaced and stoic in the only photo we had of him standing in front of his cabin with his family. The cabin was blown away in the great brushfire/sandstorm predating the Dust Bowl by several years. The Raging Winds, as they were known. After the Raging Winds, he took the family to Alberta, worked that soil for several years, and then returned alone to Minnesota, where he scouted mindlessly for a bit of land he could afford; he was most certainly suffering from dementia and starvation when he fell in the bog hole. When he was revealed by the blade of the motorized peat-gathering machine (the desire of a man named Al Wildberg to compete with the soft coal industry), he was bisected neatly, head to toe. Wildberg decided it would cut into his gathering schedule too much to call anyone to see yet another bog man. He gave Uncle Stan a firm kick with his boot, watched his arm crumble to dust, kicked him a few more times, and then got into his machine, cranked it up, gave it a bit of choke, and ran over Ramrod Man.

6

I'm unconvincing as a bog man. A small twist in my smile betrays me to Thompson. My body is facing northeast along its vertical axis in order to throw the Ohio State archaeology team a loop if they come, so that they'll conjure up some sacrificial rite to the spring rain gods. We bog folk often attempt the best we can to make some pretense of history (thus my arm thrown dramatically back and the Hamletesque thoughtfulness of my brow line); my demeanor must be that of the hard-bitten down-on-his-luck soul handpicked for sacrifice. An easy role for me, I admit.

Thompson proceeds to clear my entire ear, around the bottom of my jaw, while twilight smears the western flank of his farm, darkens the thick crowns of his windbreak. He's talking softly to me, his voice modulating with the breeze. It takes me a second, but then I realize that he's making a confession, and it's about Irene in the tobacco shop.

Sure she's young, sure, a kid, really. But lovely to behold. So lovely. And along with her girl-smells, perfume and the like, she always smells like a fresh pouch of rough cut.

Before that he said: I did, do love Alice. She's a fine woman and mother to my children—yet there's something in her, well, I guess a demeanor is the word. We don't mix. Oil and vinegar. We worked this land side-to-side during the great '67 hardships, the Great Wind of '88, the Dry Spell of '89, the Cricket Plague of '90, and all the little plagues in between, but that's not enough, to have toiled through some rough times is not enough at all. Those irrigation pipes were her idea. I'd have to admit that much.

Then: Smelled like pipe tobacco, she even admitted it and we laughed and took a turn out in her car—one of those little compact Japanese deals—to the lake, where I must admit we kissed a long, long time, first one, first time, a kiss lasting a good twenty minutes minimum.

He leans down to whisper this fact into my ear, tapping it softly with the tip of his trowel.

Slipped me the tongue, he whispers, his voice gaunt and tight. She was up here at the house—snuck up one night—and we were on the sleeping porch and the house was quiet behind us and we were on the hammock I have back there and that's when it happened, my dear bog friend, when I went over onto the other side of sin and salvation and found myself in the darkness . . . but here his confession waned. He had reached that point we all reach when the desire to speak the truth meets up with the pain it produces.

Carefully he dug out around the northern side of my head, working gently in the darkness. Night swallows dipped through the sky. The first stars emerged. I saw Lyra for the first time in years. The Big Dipper. The Little Dipper. Polaris nailed the whole spinning arrangement down and gave me a sense of orderly circular motion.

7

Arriving from Ohio State and points east (Harvard had a fine bog team), pulling up in station wagons (with the OSU logo), professional types in horn rims and chinos speaking in baroque accents, they would examine me reverently, find the tuberculous infection in my spine that caused my hunchback (yes, folks, I suffer certain deformities). Eventually they'd order a crane in, box me with sheets of steel on all sides, and heft me skyward. They'd look up at me in their absurd orange hard hats. The chief bog guy, Scrunk, would stop and promise Thompson full visitation rights. You'll be given full credit for the find, he'd say. You found Elyria Man. Who? Elyria Man. Here he'd point up at me. In the historical record, Scrunk would get full credit for the name coinage. He'd get all the glory.

If the Ohio State people came, I'd tell them to get off my farm, Thompson says eagerly. His voice is soft and wispy and clearly not directed at me or even at some imaginary Scrunk but, for the most part, at himself.

That's what I'd end up saying to them, he quickly adds. He's tapping a finger firmly against the leather of my cheeks the way you might play a bongo drum.

8

Tollund Man lay still a good two thousand years. Tollund Man—contrary to opinion—had a forlorn look, and didn't much like being dug up, either. He was resting nicely—after some sheep-counting and some concentration exercises, after stretching a charley horse out of his right leg. Sound sleep. Deep sleep. When the peat diggers came upon him he felt the way you might feel waking up on a hot, humid morning after bathing in dream-sweat all night. You try waking up in a fen, in the dead heat of a summer midmorning after a good two thousand years' rest with a noose of rope around your neck, and see how you feel. Tollund never got over it. He'd be quick to point out that he had to deal with the Danish police, too, who accused him of being a murder victim.

In Thompson's field, I could relate to Tollund Man.

9

I used to be well acquainted with this bog girl resting silently up in the scrub pines overlooking Lake Michigan from St. Ignace. She's up there waiting, as is the wont of all of us, to be exhumed, revealed. Her wrists are tied with yellow nylon tow rope. She's the albino white of subterranean cave dwellers.

The wings unfolding from her spine are the petrified remains of her rucksack. She had one of those neat army-issue sacks that matched her fatigue pants and her commando jacket—the same one she said her brother brought back from the war. Her fine blond hair is twirled up into what seems to be an ancient Swabian knot, held secure by a little leather hook and a wooden needle. The serenity of her face reminds one of Joan Baez when she was singing one of her protest songs. The position of her body in relation to the north-south axis, facing the lake, indicates that a drug rite might have transpired. A cheap nickel zodiac symbol (Libra) adorns her neck.

10

Coincidentally, Thompson grew up near the bog girl in Michigan, not far down the road, just above the bridge past rinky-dink tourist traps meant to look like authentic Indian lodges. She was just another trippy barefoot tourist girl up from Chicago, hiking the spur line that cupped Little Traverse Bay, smoking doobies with the townies. She had a worldly, assured bounce to her walk and was the first girl he'd met who had fringe on her bell-bottoms and smoked hash, not grass.

11

My old man would take this hat box down from the closet and remove this skull and hold it out to me and say he was going to do the same thing to my head if I didn't shape up, Thompson's saying. He stops for a moment to light his pipe, drawing the big flame down into the bowl. Thompson is versed in the art of maintained pipe smoking, packing the bowl just right and drawing the correct amount of air to keep it lit for an hour. Old man hit the Jap with his bayonet, thrust and twist, as he liked to say. He'd go around the house saying it over and over. Thrust and twist. Thrust and twist. Hand-to-hand on Iwo. Chopped it clean off for trophies. Lots of the men did that. Bleached it, dragged it behind the ship to let the fish pick it clean, packed it up and shipped it home to wife back in the States. Even showed me this photo of a woman and her skull in *Life* magazine.

For a second I worry. I imagine Thompson decapitating my bog head and carrying it around in a bowling bag like Perseus, appropriating my protective powers.

12

With the sky overhead I conjure a bog dream: my intact genetic material will provide a full history—tooth formation (gnarly); propensity for gallstones; rectal fissures; cancerous skin, liver. They take the stored genetic material and clone me. Elyria Man, thin, wan, with a hankering for stimulants, narcotics, and with a propensity for finding solitude, for thriving on solitude, for sleeping in haylofts, for hiding from the police. Gaunt and deprived-looking no matter how much food is brought to me. A smoker, too, taking long solemn drags on the cigarettes, pipes, cigars, bongs. I'll be known as the E. man, yet another clone product escaped from the lab in Cleveland.

13

In what seems like necrophilia, Thompson sheds his work pants—in the semidark—thinking, as he does so, of Irene's lithe body swinging softly beneath her overalls. She's coming over later. He gave the secret sign at the tobacco store. He broke the airtight seal of the packet of Captain Black. If I break the seal then it's a sign, okay, we'll agree on that, it means you've got to come out to the farm and see me, as soon as you finish up work. In his crotch he feels the imminent twang of her arrival. But he's also thinking of Isaiah, of those words imparted by the great prophet, "Enter into the rock, hide thee in the dust, from before the terror of the Lord, from the splendor of his majesty." He's down in the hole with his palm cupped gently around my jaw, feeling the glossy skin beneath my chin.

14

We killed her, Thompson's admitting to me. Years back, back when I was just a kid and Jason and I were playing around, it got out of hand, I guess that's the best way to put it, and one thing led to another; that's how it felt, at least, but I don't remember much, just the rope, the bright yellow rope. We were tripping and it was like, wow, check out that yellow rope. We stole it off her father's boat, the line and the water skis, too. A fine pair of wooden skis. He had a hell of a boat, an old Chris Craft with those deep, dark wooden sideboards that used to tear up and down Walloon Lake. Jason was wild on the skis, kicking one off, leaping the wake. Then she went out, I remember. We opened it up full-throttle. Then she went down and Jason swung back around to find her and tore right over her. A messed-up, drug-induced error was all it was, the kind of thing that happened all the time back then. We didn't know that. We didn't know a thing. And she was a rich girl with a Chicago lawyer father. All the tow ropes were bright yellow back then. Later, in the seventies, they were blue, then orange in the eighties.

His breath touches my ears. The drums tingle, the words of his confession swing against the tympanic membrane—we bog folk have well-preserved tympanic membranes—all the way round the semicircular canal, that glorious spiral formation.

15

Thompson comes out into the field with a large shovel, glances around in all four directions, and then begins covering me up, starting first with my legs, then working up to my gut, and eventually, somewhat reluctantly, covering my neck. Finally, after smoking a bowl of Captain Black, he covers my eyes. Then he packs the dirt down over my eye sockets, tamping gently with the flat of the blade. Admittedly, the rush I feel being buried again and relieved of my own earthly burdens is somewhat, but not exactly, sexual in nature. In an oversexed climate one might describe the sensation as orgasmic. That would be a failure of my descriptive powers. But they fail me now.

Back in the barn Thompson hitches the plow to the tractor and roars out. Up and down he goes, matching the furrows. Whenever he plows or combines or tills or fertilizes, he visualizes his field as John Glenn might see it up in space: the neat furrows aligned in a beautiful geometric arrangement.

16

Irene shows up around ten, hitching her thumbs into the front of her overalls and swaying her hips as she steps through the field. The wind has died and left behind a soft residue of manure smell in the air, as rich and fragrant as anything in the world. He takes his Maglite out and slaps it against his palm to get it to burn steady and swings the orb around as if searching for me and then, finally, after looking a while, holds her hand, and he says, Oh shit I must've plowed the guy under, I can't believe it, I decided to neaten up the furrows and I was listening to Bach, I mean you know how I am when I'm tuning into some fine music behind the wheel. It was somewhere around here, for Christ's sake, he says, kicking the dirt a couple of times for good measure.

17

She doesn't really believe his story, not exactly, and detects a tremor of dishonesty when he claims he accidentally buried the bog man, plowed him under. He was talking about this bog guy, she'll tell her best friend June. He kept going on and on about it. Said it was this guy maybe a million years old, maybe a thousand. I just sat there and listened to him, at the store, and then he wanted me to come out and see it and it wasn't there. Said he buried it, but I'm sure he was fibbing. He scratches his ear when he lies.

But that night in the field she made an inventory of those things she found attractive: the hair on his chest has that middle-age thickness, speckled gray. The simple unassuming way he moves through his house; upstairs, making little two-step dance movements naked in the center of the room, raising his hands up and spinning around. The husky nature of his laugh, coming easy out of her feeble jokes. Standing before him she felt polished, smoothed against his roughness. He seemed to deeply appreciate the youth of her own body. He held her so that her nipples just touched his chest and the rest of her felt suspended in midair. She liked the boyish rounded edges he presented, the flesh around his ass flat and white; above his rear a small fine patch of hair downy and soft. Good for nuzzling. For hugging. For holding her softly. And his fingers seemed even now after making love several times to still be finding and negotiating their way around her thighs and legs, not just out of shyness but some deeper, innate respect for her body. He was a good fuck, she told June. Simple as that. The guy knew what he was doing. He was king. He made her come and come again. Yeah, he's old enough to be my dad and he says it just about every time we get together, but so what, I need a dad, didn't have one, and well that's what I need and that's what he has to offer. She adds to her list: his fatherly tone, not patronizing but kind of a soft shuffle as he offers up suggestions on how to approach this fucked-up world. Ask that manager of yours for a raise, he said. You practically run that show. Without you, Kennel would be lost; he doesn't know his Symphony from his Borkum Riff. Tell him you'll buy a percentage of his store. Don't ask him. Offer it up like you're doing him a favor. Assume you're buying in. If he says no, then give him a nice little threat. Tell him you've got your eye on that vacant storefront on Maple that would make a hell of a great smoke stand. He'll say we don't have room for another smoke store. Tell him we got room for one with a walk-in humidor and a cute girl behind the counter. That's my advice to you, young lady.

18

The aquifers have dropped to all-time lows. The irrigation pumps have run dry and fried out. On the television weather map, a big fat sun stays pasted to the Midwest. Thompson mentions me again in passing, to John, his Amish friend, trying to cast some blame for the drought. The drought started right after I dug up and then accidentally buried that bog man, he says in the street one afternoon.

Softly and discreetly John chews his tobacco plug, gently flexing his jaw, a bit of juice showing on his teeth, and then spits sidelong into the gutter. Could've figured that out myself, he says, adjusting the brim of his hat with two fingers. The Lord don't have a need of us to go digging the dead out of the soil any more than the living should be climbing down into the dirt. He speaks with a deliberation that seems weighted by the illogic of his thoughts. His thoughts are heavy with faith. The leadenness of believing so fully in something like a god, something you can't see or taste or touch. Yeah, right, Thompson says, cutting him off. Well, I guess it's pretty obvious what's causing the dry spell. He gives John a nod, touches the bill of his cap, and walks down to the tobacco shop. Inside, the sweet aroma of tobacco and magazine paper mixes with the cool of the air-conditioning. Irene is behind the counter popping cigarette packs into a plastic rack, pushing them back against the spring-loaded device so that, later, when she removes them for customers she'll feel the next pack snap urgently into place. In front of the magazines the men, mostly dressed in loose black trousers, white shirts, and suspenders, are staring into their reading materials, covers folded over covers.

Thompson stands for a moment and imagines what he might do to shake things up, to send a small tremor over the peaceful, almost pastoral nature of their yearning. You know, bog folk would fit neatly into your desires, he might argue with them. The wet, smooth skin resembling what was once alive but isn't anymore succumbing to the grotesqueries of skin and orifices and the splaying of legs. You'd stare deep into the wild grimaces of Tollund Man, the supplicate, almost matronly lips of Roum Woman, the tiny haunches of Falster Boy, his throat slit from ear to ear. You'd gaze long at Windeby Girl in her tight blindfold. At Bocksten Man snuffed and staked to the ground like a pup tent, you'd gape. They'd listen to him as he spoke and nod and chew their tobacco and say, Yeah, you're Elyria Man for certain, and by virtue of being found around here, we'd have to say you're one of us.

But instead of speaking, Thompson goes to the counter—white from coin scratches—and watches his own hands rest there while Irene, dressed today in a white blouse and tweed skirt outfit that seems matronly and formal, reaches back without looking and intuitively rests her hand on the golden pouch of tobacco.

[THE PROJECT]

Maybe it was with a strange kind of reverence—of the monk toward his god—that I decided on my quest to stake out and occupy each province of my household. My duty was to seek out each spot in the house, to locate the ones that I hadn't made fully mine, and to go to those places and spend enough time in them to know them completely. This was how I came to be found under the desk one night by Jenny, who upon noticing me there gave a startled yelp (she was sitting down to write another letter to a councilman about the property tax situation, which is beyond all control—her words—and must be changed because our property is assessed for much more than its actual value. We pay more than our due, she says; it's a theme with her). She found me under the desk when her toes touched my foot. I was all the way to the back of the desk, as

far back as I could get, hunched up, examining mostly the carpet—a yellow shag—and the flanks of the desk's legs, around
which paper clips and pencils had collected back there along
with dust balls and insect frass, or what I construed to be insect frass, although I had no way of authenticating it because
I am no expert. Jenny did not know about my project. She believed I was searching for a piece of paper that had slipped
back there, as papers are prone to do, or plugging in a computer cable, or just looking for termite damage. There were
small piles of sawdust everywhere, and this gave me a pretext
on which to begin my adventure—it shielded me for a few
months, until it became evident to Jenny that I was one hundred percent committed to the project. Until then I was able
to commit myself to each spot. I selected them in the morning
over a cup of orange juice. I listed them on the yellow pad,
which I kept locked in the strongbox under the bed upstairs
(we were sleeping in separate rooms at that time, not simply in
single beds, as in old television episodes, but separate rooms allowing us each our own peculiarities and quirks, going
through the door between the rooms when we felt like copu-
lating, which was about twice a week). The list was never finished, but I began it knowing that the project would be one
that grew upon itself—the exact biological phrase eludes me
now—and the next spot, the intake vent for the furnace in
Dodge's room: a large metal grille with a brown enamel finish, was one that required me to lie down, face against the
grille, for a good twenty minutes to get the particularities of
that vantage down specifically, which I did. It was, I might

add, more compelling than the spot under the desk (although here I must add that there were many other spots in and around the desk that needed careful checking); consolidated on the inner inside edge of the box pipe, at the point where the duct made a right angle into a rectangle of pure darkness, the lint and dust and carpet fibers and dead skin of the house had collected into a ridge at which I stared for ten minutes to get down all of its qualities; there were bits of toys, too dust-covered to afford an exact ID, but I could make out that they were action figures of the small variety, like the mummified Pompeiians. I'd order Jenny to go at them with a couple of un-wound coat hangers, tweezer them up and out of there (if they went in, they'll come out) and wash them with care, and present them to Dodge as something lost and now found, to draw from him the raw delight he gets at the appearance of a new toy, or of an old one lost for days (years in his time) under the couch. When he sees a toy resurrected before his eyes, he'll often squeal and dance wildly about in an aboriginal manner, twisting his body. Before I proved to be one hundred percent committed to the project, in the weeks when I was still some-what ambivalent about keeping the yellow-pad record of my ventures, I often used the original source of the mission—examining the house for signs of the termites—as an excuse to dig into places that were of little interest and held my gaze for no more than twenty or thirty minutes, such as down in the basement, in the little crawl space beneath the front entry-way—prime for bugs, snug against raw earth, offering them ample entry for their foraging white bodies. There was little to see except for the substructure of the porch thatched over by planking, and slices of white sunlight coming in through cracks from the street, disturbed and broken up by the movement of people. While I watched, Dodge passed back and forth, playing alone, his little murmurs barely audible enough to identify. He made sounds like a dove or a nightingale (although for the life of me I've never heard a real nightingale and wouldn't know one if it were whistling in my ear), babbling mostly in his own language; back and forth, he broke up the slices of light until Jenny came out and called him in to lunch and I saw her legs pass over the slits, or what I had to presume were her legs, or her ankles, moving through the light, and then Dodge, too, and then nothing but long graceful dust-moted angles coming into the rubble floor of the crawl, against my cheek—or one cheek, to be specific, because to get in there I'd had to wiggle and waggle and snake, leaving my feet out in the basement itself. Two hours that observation took, yielding me little, on the pretext of a termite hunt, though I did find a spot, flaking off a fine top layer of wood and making out in one slim band of light their milky bodies spilling against each other—an opportune find, really, because behind me Jenny was tugging at my shoe and asking me to come to lunch and wondering if I'd found any bugs, and I was able to say yes I had and to even let her look in and see the eaten spot. Now, a few days later, I venture into the garage, to the rotted baseboard along the south wall. A long vestige of dry rot leads to the corner, where water is seeping in and a small mushroom has bloomed; there are little shells of dead in-

sects that require the utmost observation and seem so numer-
ous as to be uncountable, but count them I must, I conclude,
because it seems as if the project depends on the closest of
scrutiny and an accounting of everything; whether I, for that
matter, am fully up to the task is a question I can ill afford to
ask, but ask it I do, on my knees on the cold concrete with
only a slim light through the window, blocked by a great
clump of brambles and allowing past only a dry, dusty afternoon light. There are sounds outside conspiring to muddle me.
My name as it is called repeatedly by both Dodge and Jenny
sounds for all the world like the name of someone who has
been lost for hours in a cold, dark sea, a raging sea: the name
of a man who is suffering from hypothermia and can hardly
clutch at the lifeline that has been thrown, his fingers slipping,
the sizzling spray of the rotor blades blinding him. It's the way
you'd call someone who has been dead for hours, I think, but
then I must be deceiving myself, because they have—I am
sure—thrown their full support behind me in this project,
vowed to support me to the end, and I've laid it out before
them in the clearest terms. I'm here, I call back, still counting,
not willing to take my eyes from the pill bugs and millipedes,
the dry husks of their forms, shelled and sucked empty of life.
I'm here, I'm here.

[HUNGER]

As soon as she heard it again from Jimmy's lips in the social service office, waiting in line, lines, lines, and more lines—like man if we don't qualify for some real monies, we got to like hit one of the houses up on the ridge—she knew exactly which one, a raised ranch with about five sets of sliding doors just dying to be jimmied. The old retired codger was always out on his lawn with his putter, practicing shots while she and Jimmy scraped around in the brush spying on him; tall crabgrass, little alcoves in the weedy meadow where they set up campfires with other rejects. Year in, year out since high school they'd partied there; now new houses were encroaching, plots marked out in yellow ribbons, foundations setting in wooden forms (they'd done their best to mess around with those but found the wood glued to the hardened concrete);

there were skeletal superstructures worth torching if the escape route out—a single little dirt utility road—weren't so chancy. Sliding glass doors, cheap dead bolts, the house was awaiting Jimmy's lock-picking swiftness. (He'd been a locksmith apprentice and was as fast at picking as an average Joe was at inserting a key and turning the tumblers; he knew the kinks in the major lock brands: Yale, Jiffy, and Quicktight, the particular one dominating market share, found on just about every door on every home. He knew that most doors could be kicked in with a single, Zen-directed blast of the boot heel.)

It's a plan. It's a sure, fuckin' thing, it's rigged, we're set, were gonna go in that back sliding door, they spoke softly, back in the bushes, eyeing the dark house. Over the roof the stars pierced the dark. The tingle of dope smoke slept on their tongues; in the pit of their stomachs—along with the vacuum of fear—lay a deep munching hunger that belied all their sorrows and seemed to be a hunger for much more than just nutritional substance. I could eat God, the hunger said. I could eat the universe. From that point on, stepping forth across the lawn to that back door, it stood there before them fully formed—as a scheme—because, sure as sure was sure, as Jimmy said, they'd have to tie the old coot up and maybe stuff an old sock in his mouth to keep him from making noise—not that there could be a soul for miles who could hear it, more for the general morale, the style of the thing. There were prescripts behind even the sloppiest break-in job, and Jimmy and Janet had them down pat, although most of what they'd done in the past by way of stealing stuff had been knee-jerk, spur-of-the-moment rip-offs of close friends: for example, once in the dead of winter they'd found themselves at a church camp along the lake, a collection of boarded cabins huddling around a main log lodge with a tarp-covered pool and a tennis court. That heist included a booty of old *Holy Bibles* and *Pilgrim Hymnals*, which fueled their campfire—tossed in one by one— for thirty minutes. Burning books was good fun. It was a joyous thing. The way the pages curled into the flames, the thin, brittle paper, the word reduced to carbon. A twenty-gallon can of peaches in a storage room took fifteen minutes to open with a hand opener, only to reveal them rotting and gooey in sugar syrup. Hefting it down the trail, they poured the goop all over the tennis court, watching it harden and steam in the crystalline air.

Surprise was the basic element of a break-in (you surprise them; they surprise you). Jimmy looked forward to scaring the coot, to seeing fear glaze his eyes, to getting right up to his old puckered mouth—breath wheezing in and out—and frightening him out of the depths of his sleep. What does an old fuck dream about, anyway? he was thinking as he walked across the yard, upon which the moonlight threw a thin veneer of frosty light on the grass blades. Janet was right beside him but might as well have been in England, for all he knew, because he was going into one of his singular trances, a fugue state driving him to that door, which he'd jimmy with a little flick of his screwdriver; the wooden security bar might be in place in the groove, but he knew a hard yank back on most of these doors would jolt it right out of the runners. If that didn't work, he'd resort to a blast with his boot heel, noise be damned. Old men must dream in old-think, dreams slow and soggy and worthless, the hardness gone out of their bodies. His old man had been that way, sagging under the weight of years and booze. The idea would be to scare the piss out of this one, to watch him firm up in fright, and to get a good laugh out of it before the sock went into his mouth.

∴

Where are we? Where are we? Where are we? Where are we? Where are we? Where are we? Where are we? Trying not to listen, he got the corkscrew into the cork, enjoying the feel of it as it jabbed in, the point easing into the softness. It's the speed, he thought, but he wasn't sure because she'd blindly groped a couple of the little numbers out of the Ziploc bag in the dark and then downed them dry, hacking away. When the cork broke off, he said fuck, and jammed it down into the bottle, raised the neck, and slugged down several deep gulps—bitter and briny—and then spat the flecks of cork out the window into the night. Paw Paw, Michigan, wine. Bitter and briny.

I said where are we?

It seems we're at the fish hatchery, he said.

They were.

You sick, Godless fuck, the frail voice spoke from someplace, most likely in his brain. (His standard-issue hallucinatory voice: a tight, Middlewestern twang combined with the intonations of Franklin Roosevelt.)

Shut up, he commanded his voice.

What? she said, squirming in her brown suede jacket with fringe, a white T-shirt stained with sweat. She claimed to have some Indian blood—or he thinks she said something about it when they met on the porch at the clinic, but he's not sure. Might as well have some blood. Long, dark hair like one, skin like one.

You shut up, he said, jerking to the backseat in a manner that indicated he was hearing his standard-issue voices again.

You're hearing it again, she said.

Standard issue, he said.

When you kill someone you're left with a jellylike residue spread across your soul, he remembers some guy telling him at the clinic; they were in a circle, shifting on their haunches, trying to avoid hemorrhoid flare-up from the folding chairs, talking, topping each other, trying like hell to put on a good show before Howard the shrink came in and they'd have to taper off; nothing they said was supposed to be held against them in any court of law, but you never knew because the world was shifty and you could get shafted by anyone in the universe; the guy talking about the jelly had killed several kids, or claimed he had, and buried them in an old dry well, or a cistern, or some such place in a farmstead out in Kansas, or maybe one of the Dakotas, North or South. He told his story with deliberate nonchalance. When you kill someone this jelly stuff coats you and you have to wash it off like skunk smell with a solution of vinegar and salt. If that doesn't work it has to be burned off with a film of rubbing alcohol. Something like that. Then some frail little skinny twerp arsonist interrupted and launched into his long fantastic voyage of burning and that was all Jimmy had a chance to remember because Janet opened the door and went outside the car, walking along the cement sluiceways of the hatchery, sucked up by the darkness. He took another long guzzle from the wine, opened the door, and stepped out to go find her. Along the huge basins loaded with fish were machines that sold food pellets. At one he stopped, took a quarter out, put it in the slot, and gave a hard twist, churning up a fistful of small pellets into his open palm. He'd walk down the sluiceway with the fish food warm in his hand, find a spot with some light to illuminate the rising fish. They'd come up like a bunch of pigs, a wild writhing show of brute hunger, all those little fish mouths sucking for the pellets, and only so many pellets to go around. He liked that, liked the stupidity of groping. A few got food. The rest could go starve for all he cared. But of course they wouldn't starve, because being a fish was a good, clean, wholesome life. Some guy came out with a basket of fresh worms, or whatever, and flung them in every afternoon. Feeding time. As far as he could see there weren't any flood lamps or even any streetlamps to speak of; just the clammy damp stench of fish mingled with the sound of the curling lip of water making its way over the gates. He liked how the glossy top, coated with algae and pollen dust, moved at a leisurely pace until it got to that little razor-blade spot where it roared over the edge. That spot. That's where he lived all the time. Right fuckin' there. Where the hell was she? The anger he'd felt earlier—snuffing out the old man—was rising again.

You're gonna stop right there and not move an inch and keep your hands out where I can see them, the voice intoned while the flashlight beam sliced around his ankles. It was the craggy voice of a dumb-fuck security guy, not a cop, he could tell, some elderly bimbo working night shifts to keep his old lady in the nursing home. He'd had enough interaction with cops and such to know that the two routes available to him were as clear-cut and precise as any: you'd either make a quick darting run for it and figure on some kind of pursuit, scrambling over fences and through brush, the cop holding off on shooting you because he's worried about lawsuits and investigations and messy stuff like that; or you go for a violent give-and-take, hand to hand at close range (close enough to make it hard for the cop to grab his gun), that might result in your death, his, or both. He figured the second course of action was the best and took the fistful of pellets, turned, faced the man, said good evening, sir, and flung them hard. They passed the man's head and landed in the water and caused a great white rush of tiny mouths—a bubbling accompaniment to the spongy thud the pipe made (he later found out it was a hunk of sprinkler piping that Janet had found along the edge of the hatchery) as it hit the old codger in the skull. Nothing on earth like the sound of lead hitting flesh, he thought. But apparently the speed or whatever Janet was on wasn't stopping there, and she gave Jimmy a slug in the head, too.

He woke up in the pure white corridor of the Elma General Hospital. He'd been through the process enough times to know how it went: first the opening of the darkness into a small little pinpoint of white (at which point he pretty much knew what was going on because there were the little PA calls of Dr. Such-and-Such will you please go to such-and-such ward. Such-and-such nurse, please come to such-and-such station, along with the crying, begging, and pleading (or the hallowed silence) of his fellow emergency roommates. Then the widening of the pinhole to the bright white of the crystalline neon lights, at which point he'd close his eyes to avoid the rest, the face looking down at him in concern, asking his name, asking it again and again and again until he spit it forth, adding asshole to the end: Jimmy Turner, asshole. Then from there, days and days in critical care without a television, the ten bucks rental fee not covered by The State. No one except the medical staff and a single welfare guy from The State would come to visit. He'd been through it before and would most likely go through it again, but this time it seemed drawn out. It took up his life. It took up a great deal of his entire life while in the outside world Janet went off on a wild hike over the sand traps and fairways of the dark golf course adjacent to the hatchery, and then slept off the pills in a clump of brush, while the old codger security guy suffered his concussion and severe memory loss, waking hard-pressed to put a face to the guy he'd confronted (and it was all smothered in the half-light and darkness anyhow).

Janet took the car (keys still in the ignition) and drove to Elma Park, her central headquarters, and there she avoided cops and found new friends and did her best to completely forget Jimmy (because it had dawned on her after five minutes of staring at her friend, sprawled on the ground next to the hatchery tank, that maybe she had made a grievous error in giving him such a hard pop with such a hard pipe). The loot from their exploits that evening disappeared into the hands of a dealer, who in turn gave her a small baggie loaded with white-comet life-force powder.

∴

Just the faintest sound of footfalls on the thick carpet padding, a lingering give of floorboard along with the central air sealed silence of the house to keep the sound of crickets out. He was an old man but not particularly weak. He worked out on his home gym, kept his muscles toned, and during his life he had put in his time doing manual stuff, putting a shovel tip into the ground alongside the other men, even when he was doing the contracting. He was proud of this fact. When he looked in the mirror and made a careful study of what was left of his physique, he saw the general sagging along his bones, the veins and arteries rising up through the rice-paper skin; the only major defect aside from age was the small scar just above his Adam's apple (he had one of those turkeylike jiggling gullets). He took pride in the faculties he had left, honed them, buffed and rebuffed. One of these was his acute auditory sense. I can hear like hell, he liked to say. I've got the ears of a dog. So when he heard the soft give of the loose stair board (the only squeaky step), he rolled sideways out of bed (because his only other affliction of account was his tight back, which would spasm in knots if it took the full lift of his body from the prone position), twisted in a half gainer, and landed softly on the carpeting, where he leaned over and groped from beneath the bed a nine-iron golf club he superstitiously kept there—not so much for protection from an intruder but because he had golfed his whole life and felt that in keeping a club there he might, when his spirit left his body and hovered momentarily, be able to reach down beneath the bed and clutch the arm of his favorite club and haul it up to heaven. There wasn't much light in the room, just the pale wash of starlight. But with his eyes adjusted he could see enough to make out the shadowy torso of the intruder in the doorway, just standing, unmoving, and then he heard the sharp intake and outtake of his breathing labored from the stairs (it was Jimmy in the doorway, not sure exactly if he was in the bedroom or a bathroom but getting the feel that it was a bedroom before discerning a movement of something in front of him. His eyes were adjusted but not 20/20, more 20/40, and a bit of cataract had formed on one eye along with whatever effects years of drug use had produced; so the form in front of him was twisted partly sidelong the way an image distorted by heat might be, and he hardly had a chance to get his bearings when there was the swish of the club and he was struck in the side, near his kidney, and knocked over). Janet came and flicked on the light. A gangly old man, knotted with muscles, his pajama shirt open, wielding a nine-iron in what seemed to be mute surprise. Usually what you expect in these cases was a loud huh, a shout, something meant to scare the intruder away. That was the scenario. Usually the victim would engage in some kind of dialogue right off, set the standards, get things in order before you tied him up to a chair and took him to the basement and then, later, after watching his eyes dart around madly and so on, blow him away with a shotgun wrapped in a towel. (As was mentioned, Jimmy had a pretty good overall sense of how these gigs worked.) Instead, the old geezer just stood silently without uttering a word and held the club side-long over his head. A strong-looking old fart when put next to Jimmy's drug-depleted form, but not so against the jittering insectlike quickness of Janet, jerking behind in the shadows. (She'd moved back into the hall after throwing the switch.) She flew forward, and in a swift Judo move, snapping her arms around his midsection while engaging his ankles with her feet, disarmed the old man and twisted him to the ground, and then engaged him in a wrestling match. The thick carpeting pro-vided ample padding for this occasion; it induced the wrestling, she later thought, much later, when details were few and far between: the club glinting over his head, the thick, heavy sheen of its wooden shank, the brass-coated read-ing lamps on both sides of the bed, a night table littered with brown pill bottles, capped in light blue, a mother lode of pre-scription heart pills and sleeping aids. (They'd load those up into one of the old guy's socks and take it along to the hatch-ery.) The wrestling match moved along elegantly in the Greco-Roman style, with headlocks and half nelsons and quick leg movements, and while they went at it, Jimmy, not wanting to ruin a good moment, began to pilfer the room, going first to the closet, looking under the shoes, work boots, slippers, high heels, sandals, flip-flops, and in the pockets of the coats hung there.

∴

How the old guy got hold of the device during the wrestling match was still a mystery to her, and to Jimmy, who was finally released from the hospital on a cold fall day and met up with Janet in the park, the bandage limp from his forehead, blaming his injury for the loss of details. The old coot must've reached up onto the nightstand to get it during the wrestling. She didn't see it. It was shaped a bit like a gun, but more like one of those German electric razors, and when he turned it on it sounded like a razor, and she was sure it was a razor until he held the buzzing instrument up to his throat and began to make words out of the vibration, one at a time, having to press it deep into the flesh to get the sound out of his throat. His dentures were out and his gums had a hard time working into the proper shape. For a year he had trained in the use of the device, and part of the training was learning a whole new scheme for shaping the mouth around the words. In doing so, he had learned the essence of what it is we do when we speak. How much is involved.

Each word is a small miracle of air and shape. Each word urges itself upon the mouth. Each word is sacred.

Stop, he said.

Jesus Christ, Jimmy said, coming around. Over his arm was a green sport coat and a plaid pair of golf pants.

It's fuckin' Helen Keller.

Take what you want and be on your way, the buzz said.

The disappointment Jimmy felt over this sudden development was acute; that his original intention of stuffing a sock in the old man's mouth—in lieu of duct-taping it the way they did in most of the flicks—had been thwarted. The plan had called for a sock and now here was an old fuck who had to put an electric razor to his throat to buzz the words out like a robot.

∴

Sitting on the carpet with the buzzer in his hand, the man had a flashback: a few weeks after the house was finished and the poured patio had hardened (because as a mason he refused the standard-issue wooden deck of treated wood and even worked alongside the men as they poured the patio, to make sure the concrete was kept properly wet and set correctly) and his belongings were unpacked and put in place, he went outside and sat in his lawn chair. When he was alone he often tried to speak without the machine, just mouthing the air. Inside his head he could hear those words. But this afternoon he felt the urge to hear something, so he put the machine to his throat and buzzed a few bars of the "Moonlight Sonata," just a hum, and then sang a little bit of Sinatra, and in doing so he remembered the way it had felt to smoke all of those cigarettes while working, doing some underpinning of a house, digging out beneath the footing, laying frames, guiding the chute into place and making the hand sign to the driver to begin the pour—all that cool clumped grayness slushing down the chute while he sprayed it with the hose, slushing it into place, waiting to be smoothed. All that hard work, and then, as a reward, a moment of silence as the smoke slips across his throat. Now it was replaced with the buzz. Not the same thing, he thought; but somehow similar.

∴

Take what you want and don't hurt me, the buzz said. Hearing this standard-issue plea filled Jimmy with an intense wariness. In the space behind his skull, the voices began a Greek chorus. No buzz in those fucking voices. Singing a kind of lullaby, he later said to himself, or maybe it was to one of the doctors in the clinic a few years later when he was back in, trying to get his life in order and cleaned up but not admitting, of course, to what he had done that night. It wasn't a demon chorus. Not of his own making. Not of his own doing.

We should take off. This isn't right. We're off the mark here, she was saying.

She's just testing the waters of goodness when what you want, man, is to get all sticky with the death and smear it over you like grape jam, the chorus sang.

The docs at the hospital had prescribed doses of Thorazine (that classic old-time voice killer) along with the usual cocktail of lithium and all that. He spurned that stuff. He did his gig with those drugs and then let them go to the wayside. Too much planning, charting. Too many time obligations. Each day you had to pop the dose on cue. One didn't want to keep appointments with Dixie cups and rattling pills—like the tails of snakes.

He yanked the device from the old coot, kicked him in the shoulder, and fondled it, a shivering gerbil of compact machinery. When he held it up to his own throat, letting the vibration go through his voice box, the chorus slipped beneath the buzz and dissolved into the empty hiss of the air-conditioned air coming through vents, and the silence of the man on the carpeting.

He took the razor device into the bathroom, flicked on the light, and let it clatter onto the cold white floor.

Back out in the room Janet cowered on the bed, hands over her face, bowed before the situation, muttering softly, this is ill, she said, the guy can't even talk, the guy's got a fucking fucked throat, nudging the man who lay on the floor, quivering softly; his thighs extended out of pale blue boxer shorts; the muscles inside seemed to be going crazy, spasms of tension. He was trying to speak, making the best of the situation, doing what he could by way of twisting his mouth into an assortment of shapes. But all that came out was an airless huffing sound. Behind Jimmy's earlobes one of the choir members sang: You're no lip-reader. You with your own deformed mouth (he had a slight harelip) that would be hard-pressed to make a natural-sounding word; you who have forsaken and been forsaken.

∴

A featherweight. He was all skin and the frail hollow bones of a bird, tiny ribs beneath papery skin. Jimmy folded him up, not bothering to lift him off the carpet, and pulled him to the doorway so he could watch, because that's what you did, make the poor soul watch when you did shit, Jimmy figured. Expand the misery of the world by spreading it around; double your pain. Triple it. Help it build upon itself. He raised his boot up high over the buzzing device, which shivered on the tile floor. He held it there. He waited. He wanted something, a grunt, a small sigh. Raised boot heel, all potential havoc, two feet over the device. The old man moved, started to jump for it, but before he could get there—just a finger around the base of the thing—Jimmy stomped down and felt the glorious crack of the shell, aluminum-coated plastic with rubber nubs. He ground his heel into the mess of parts.

Then, sorry to say, he pretty much did the same to the old man.

On the bed Janet sat, jouncing her heels up and down in a fluttering motion that bespoke the drug-induced trauma that her nerves were under. There was something sad in the sight of her like that on a stranger's bed. Seeing her, Jimmy felt a great welling sensation come up from his chest and enter his shoulders and head. The next thing to do would be to loot the house, to turn it over, as they said, to make use of the situation the best they could and then go someplace—maybe the fish hatchery—to count the booty and to drink; that was the sensible thing to do, he said out loud. We've got to get some sense into this setup, he said, moving around the room, opening the sock drawer and finding a box of cuff links, a little packet of business cards—pulling the card out and reading:

MALCOLM HAYWOOD INDUSTRIES

Malcolm Haywood, President

Fine Masonry

888 Hill Street

NO JOB TOO LARGE OR SMALL

At the back of the drawer, rolled tight in the end of a sock, he found what he was looking for, a big stash of what seemed to be ancient coins. Booty. Old gold pieces, too, enough to conclude the robbery, enough to take with them to give a sense of completion to the mission, he told himself, and anyway the jitters that were tearing through Janet were getting profoundly violent. She seemed unable to control the movement of her arms, which were making great birdlike flaps. She was flying down the stairs, muttering about the incorrect nature of hurting an old man who couldn't talk. She felt the buzzing at the base of her ears and inside her skull. I'm afraid, she said. I'm afraid. I'm afraid. I'm afraid. I'm afraid. I'm afraid, she said again in the kitchen, opening the fridge, finding it empty except for a single pint of slaw and a large container of buttermilk. I'm afraid what we did was the incorrect thing. I mean, we shouldn't have, it's gonna haunt us, like, like maybe it's going to like haunt us, I mean, like, because the guy couldn't talk, man, couldn't talk. He didn't have his say.

But out in the woods she felt better, leaving that house behind, all the lights blazing. I feel better, she said. The car was still there, old and beat-up but looking perfectly fine in the starlight. It had moved slightly, a few yards to the west, in their absence, she was sure. The car moved, she said. The fucking car moved. The car moved. It did indeed, Jimmy said, just to assure her, as he opened the door and reached into the back where the bottles of Paw Paw wine lay nestled against each other. Here, he didn't bother with the corkscrew. Instead he went out into the cold night, broke the neck of the bottle on a rock, and lifted the broken end to his lips, taking a long draw, leaning against his car for support. In the shadows on the other side, mercifully out of sight, Janet started to make her flapping motions, as if readying herself for some long migration out of this world into the next, lifting her arms slowly, not so jauntily, making long, graceful sweeps in the air. Jimmy's wine was smooth and glassy and landed in his gut like radiator coolant, and he felt good with the heavy sock tucked into his belt, hanging, flapping down against his thigh. We'll go over to the fish hatchery and hang out for a while, he said, and then see what we can see because at this time of night it's nice there. Words were just coming up and out of him. There will be stars against the long flat slabs of dark water; there will be the gurgle of the sluice gates and all of those stupid fucking hungry fish rising up in their humiliating eagerness at the food.

[COUNTERPARTS]

A) *You see her* entering her car, disappearing from sight, smooth skin and golden hair caught gossamer by the sunlight, and behind her the weedy fields leading down to Marconi Station beach (which even at that moment you surmise might be the location of a future tryst). You've got foresight, or you feel it in your bones, a kind of light-headed vision of a masculine kind; not the soothsaying know-it-all manner in which fortune-tellers ply their trade, spreading their open palms over the crystal ball, gathering voices from the ether, speaking in firm, resolute voices. Later, you'll swear you remember seeing a sprinkle of freckles—the lightly salted, barely visible type that bring out the whiteness of her skin—along the underside of her arms.

B) In a long line at the doughnut shop with the same crew you see each morning: permanent gentry mixing it up with the hotel and rental folk. Bikes line the curbside, their fat tires resting assuredly on the pavement. She stands four or five places ahead, dressed in a wraparound of some synthetic silk— dark brown and black paisley swirls—that faintly shows the outline of her bikini. You chalk up meeting her again to deeper, celestial, cosmological influences. The smell of fat cut by dark brewing coffee, mixed with the cool salt-dew air, and, even more, the flaccid stink of salt marsh, all make you aware that, if need be, you could place blame on conspiring elements, the landscape, sea foam, and plunging, hungry gulls. Flutter flutter, the heart goes. (Not long ago you were diagnosed with an overactive heart. The inflated pressure under your ribs.)

C) When she glances back, you exchange a brief pleasantry, a hello, or a head nod, but nothing more than that, because to breach the wall between you (ah, the delicate wall of the self and the private inner life along with the natural bubble of personal space) would perhaps shatter something perfect. (Isaac Bashevis Singer called it ESP.) You misread a lift of her hand, flattened into a kind of salute, and begin to wave back at her until you notice just in time that she is only sweeping away a stray strand of hair from her brow. You linger long enough—sadly, creepily—to note that she orders a sourdough doughnut and coffee, black, and buys a *New York Times* from the kid outside.

D) Attempt to exchange viewpoints, to become this woman getting into her car. You've begged a few hours away from Ron and the kids:

—I just want a little bit of time alone, not much, I just need to decompress. Not even a day, just a few hours alone with an old bedspread and a copy of Proust. You've been trying to read *Remembrance* for months, and you did read, for a moment, on the beach, with Marconi Station behind you, about the wind sweeping across the fields of corn near Champieu, reading slowly, testing the language, attempting to understand exactly what Proust was saying about the nature of memory and time, not to mention the way the wind acts as a tutelary genius. You agree: perhaps the movement of things is only mental, and getting into your car, looking up, you see a very handsome man—he could be a year or two your senior. He looks up and you exchange not what one would call a knowing look, but a look that does contain a pulse of recognition, primal, slightly fearful. He has a fine Romanesque nose and (but how could you see this!) very gentle lips, full lips, the lips of a folk singer, the lips of a man who can transpose the grief of the world into tight but paradoxically loose songs.

E) Begin tentative chitchat (in line again, a day later) regarding quality of doughnuts: the sourdough are unearthly and the regular cakes are highly irregular. Your voice is melodic and slightly cruel and investigative. Included in your discourse are weather-related comments referring to the past two weeks of glorious clear blue skies and only one day of high surf with those lonely waves rolling in, born out of some distant tropical depression. You agree that those waves were amazing (last Wednesday), something fantastic in their immensity, not to mention (and you don't) the sense you had—seeing them come in—that their history was off in the heart of the sea, and that each wave carried with it some indication of the wind's original intent. There must be—between the two of you—a clear-cut sense of the tribulations that your current conjugal states have offered up; there must be a long backlog of unresolved fights in the docket (the mention of waves might hint at these things). A pleasing sense that you have both resigned yourselves to finding love somewhere else, under specific conditions, lingers beneath your words.

F) Lucinda. Steven. Delightedly, with great ease, as if sharing a drink, carefully, with precision, you exchange names.

G) Little Maggie digs viciously with a small yellow shovel, throwing swoops of sand into the air and into your eyes; she's making soft little cries with each toss and you sense that perhaps she, too, has had enough of the whole thing. She's small for her age, delicate, prone to catching strep throat. She's had it six times in the past year and a half, and yet her tonsils—big flaring adenoids—still cling to the back of her throat because Ron refuses to have them removed (it's an outmoded procedure), and he's knowledgeable because he's an internist.

But his specialty is cardiology. I don't know shit about pediatrics, he admits. It's impossible work because the little buggers can't speak, explain themselves, I mean, it's guesswork of a sort, hit or miss. A couple of sore throats. You don't just hack the things out. Used to put a guy in traction when he had a broken femur; now you wrap the leg in fiberglass and throw a pair of crutches at the patient and send him on his way. Ron has a habit of smoothing down the two patches of hair that frame his bald spot. I'm gonna shave it all off when it gets too thin, he says.

H) Sky and sand and the backbone of the Cape cradle their movement. They are suddenly now equally matched in the world, working their way, with longer and longer throws of the Frisbee, into the proximity of two girls in blue bikinis. (They've staked out this same part of the beach for three days straight, and the kids have exchanged some opening banter.) Two sons—Adonises, my sons. You quote from what? You were teaching a play a few semesters ago that had the word Adonis—but which one was it? Was it Williams? Maybe it was Brando saying the words. No, it was Willy Loman, talking up his sons. Talking them up in a big way. Talking them up the way you'd talk up product. Maybe he's right; maybe your kids are product. And here I am, you think, watching my sons playing catch, prancing before the beauties (and they *were* the personification of beauty, all leg and body, all movement and grace and glory and flesh) and talking them up, too.

They're subtle kids, somewhat silent, sneaking softly around your tensions with Irene, who dotes on them but in a sidelong, conspiratorial way. Behind you she's fingering a magazine, following the line of your gaze at the kids. Low on her brow her straw hat keeps the sun away.

I) Think if you must about deserted Midwestern streets covered in a soft snowfall. People leaving parties—the noise behind them as they arrive into the silence of the town late at night. Think if you must of Midwestern winter evenings of yore, of bridge parties at fold-up tables; mink stoles draped over cool white shoulders; black rubber galoshes yanked tight over the polished toes of fine dress shoes.

J) Watching the drive-in movie, an updated version of *The Absent Minded Professor* in which a green unearthly goo wobbles across the screen, you think of your life as flexing green stuff generated by computer animation, yet as real as anything—of the moment—and filling Maggie with soft contralto giggles, infectious giggles. The smile your face provides in response—for her and only for her—makes your jaw hurt. Ron reaches over to touch your hand. Through his touch you are made aware that your fingers are small and delicate and fragile, and they remind you, for some reason, of the embroidery your great-grandmother stitched by hand: her house up there near Lake Huron, clapboards under the daunting gaze of northern summers, the lake glistening bits of fire from a sky bone-white with sun.

K) Your uncle found reels of Super 8 footage in the attic and had them committed to video, to the television screen: there was your father, a young kid in swim trunks dangling his feet over the edge of a dock while behind him cold Canadian waters drew back to a line of trees from which a thin twirl of smoke slithered (always a single campfire up in the tree line). Elegant on the end of the dock, the boys are firm-boned, baring themselves up against time, hair slicked back and bodies perfect. The film reel jolts to an end and is replaced by another, different time and place, different color gradients, different vacation; same hard gorgeous bodies and slicked-back hair and cold clear lake behind the dock, but this time with a Cris Craft, flag aflutter, spreading a wide wake as your father skis before a different tree line, towering spruce melding into dark blue backdrop. The reel jolts to an end, changes again, and an Indian guide (always an Indian guide, your father once explained) on his haunches pokes the tip of a twig into the smoldering coals, puffing his cheeks as he blows; behind him your regal grandmother from Toledo draws as much elegance from the scene as she can, adjusting the shoulder of her raccoon shawl. Then your father appears in the frame dressed in a plaid shirt, mirroring a thousand future ads for sportswear, blissfully letting his gaze enter the lens and the future and daring you, just daring you, to betray eternity.

L) It's those eyes—your father's on the dock in Canada—that you see in hers, when you meet on the pine swamp trail.

The brown of a polished hickory gun butt, rubbed shiny with warm beeswax.

M)—I'd like to see you again.

—Me, too.

—We'd, well, I mean we could take another hike here—I might be able to get out from under them tomorrow when they're off—they're going on some kind of excursion, it's a tourist trap thing but they love it anyway, an ocean adventure sort of deal.

—That would be great, we can walk and I'll bring something to eat.

—Your name, Lucinda, it's . . .

—After my grandmother Lucinda.

N) Growing up in Wisconsin, there was always a lake. Your father's arms around your shoulder. Stray dogs. Hardships. The small cabin in the forest north of Milwaukee; the brewery spewing steam. Trailers, shacks, cabins abandoned for the winter by summer folks. He's also from the Midwest, from Toledo. Oil refinery flames twisting tongues of fire in the sky as his father drove him home from a visit to the office. Geography, loss, failures, the sustained efforts to keep the marriage going and to keep a steady toehold. (On what? On the Seventh Commandment, he wonders. He believes in that commandment, set forth for good reason.) Yeah, certainly there are failures beneath the surface, failures of marriage, things not received, and needs not met, too. Needs of all kinds—and that power of romantic love, of course, conspiring against conjugal forces: there are those temporal elements. Sure, those are there, too.

O) At Marconi Station a few stragglers loaded with inner tubes and fold-up chairs, towels, and coolers arise from the top of the stairs like resurrected souls, their forms lit brilliantly by the low-slung sun as it sinks into the scrub pines to the west. They see two cars in the far corner. The manner in which the cars are parked—the closeness of the vehicles, the offhanded angle of one car in relation to the other—exudes cheap, ill-conceived conspiracy. In the front seat two adults grope each other, lips touching.

P) Flesh isn't enough; flesh eats you both. The desire comes from the pine swamp (your third visit), from the hollow up there where you are safe and hidden, the sense of the sea beyond the windbreak and its great insatiable turbulent continuum as it endlessly rolls into itself. The sea is eternal. We are not. The sea is forever. Touch is not. The waves are forever. My fingers are not. One thinks of those maps in science textbooks, the circular nature of the water cycle, arrows flinging up into the perfect sky and water coming down. I used to read Eugene O'Neill, he says, touching her, thinking about the rickety house at Peaked Hill Bar falling into itself and being washed into the sea.

Q) Just pulling out—the gymnastics of postcoital movements; she's working a cramp out of her calf, a sudden charley horse that sends her bucking up, her back covered with sweat and sand. Beyond the sand and pines one hears the sweet milky sway of waves washing ashore.

R) Under the pretense of going out for a gallon of milk at the minimarket in Eastham, you drive the dark roads to Lighthouse Beach, and there, under the swaths of green-white-green-white light, you locate his car.

S) Outward yearning—he's explaining in the dark car—and inward. Forces go outward, you know, like, you know, there are people who move outward with their lives. On the CD player, the Velvet Underground sing: "Coney Island Steeplechase." —Ah, what the fuck am I trying to say? He raises his voice just a bit and it flattens itself against the windshield glass. What, in, the, fuck, am I saying? He repeats, and you laugh and run the length of your palm up the inside of his shirt. —I saw Lou Reed on the train. He was going toward Poughkeepsie, on the Metro-North, he says. He looked, well, you know, he looked like Lou Reed on a train. A bit old. Riding up the Hudson River.

T) Think of Marconi Station, the plates of steel set in cement, twisted bolts clutching empty air, those remnants of the great radio apparatus—square towers spun with wire that caught hold of the *Titanic*'s SOS call. The great trappings of myth. Think of the windswept silence of winter, the tourists gone, the information station unexamined: a model of the station beneath thick Plexiglas into which someone has scratched with great care: FUCK FUCKED FUCKER. In a few years the last of the bolts and footings will slip off the eroded cliff, eagerly into the sea.

—Hey what are, I mean what are we doing? I mean what are we going to do about this? Are we going to see each other. This can't end.

—What are we, ah, I don't know.

U) The dialogue continues around the central issue, which is, of course, exactly where do you stand and how do you stand. The dialogue above (in T) is interchangeable; either of you might say either part, although the force on the balance of scales—beloved /&/ lover—must be heavier on one side. You touch her lips with the back of your hand; there is a distinctive nip in the air, the hint of fall, and off through the trees a hollow wooden banging rises as someone boards up the windows for winter. That's the house you've pinned some hope on, a quaint little saltbox that you both agree *wants* to be inhabited by lovers. It has that secretive nature you both want from an abode, hardly room for two, with a hand-painted sign adorned with honeysuckle and illegible script bearing the owner's name, or the name they've given it. Quack weed edges up to the picket fence. To hole up there all winter with tinned meat and crackers and Scotch as supplies. Firewood and flesh on flesh as fuel. Bobby pins are stuck like needles into her hair; you adjust one as you speak and it falls out and slips beneath the seat.

V) A rude sunset. A sunset quivering sadly into the flat surface of the kettle pond. You can hardly see, staring dead-on into the horizon; yet you look and look because one is inclined to gaze into the water, across it, to see the other side. Soon you're both in the water—cold but not unbearable; the drop-off is sharp. Kids down the way are swimming, tearing open the gloss. You hold her and she holds you and there is a scream down the way and an alert is passed from kid to kid that a snapping turtle is at hand. —Do they really snap, she says to you. —Hell yes, they snap like hell. You pop a pencil into their mouths and they bite right through. Do the same to your fingers, too. The kids are young, maybe six or seven, splashing and breaking apart the silence. Sadly you heft the weight of this woman—fingers along her hips. Water and buoyancy; the conspiracy of landscape and the human that comes into everything and lends itself to blame. Blame the landscape, the Cape, the sea, the water, her skin, your lips, your tongues, the sand, grace, heart, failures.

W) From inside your hood listen to your breath: cold white sound in your ears while outside the wind roars from the outer banks. Dead smack in the middle of the winter and you're there on the shore in the half-dark of dusk bracing against the gale as the nor'easter bucks up against the headlands. Behind you lies nothing but the thin spit of land, and behind that the bay holding up against the squall. As you lean forward the wind holds you enough to betray gravity, to float like a clown with his shoes nailed down. You lean and lean and then stumble over. Behind you, your wife gives a small laugh that you can't hear. The boys are up the stairs, unwilling to come down to play a role in these middle-aged high jinks. —Jesus Christ, Dad, one of them shouts, you're crazy. Like what's up with this? When you turn away from the wind—unable to breathe—Irene is on the sand making snow angels, whipping her arms and legs in and out. It's a strange motion. To see her supine like that. Arms and legs moving in congruence. It is slightly holy, you think. It is here right now that you'll confess your infidelities. It is here in this moment that you'll tell her the whole story.

X) Miracle babe, the substance, smoking a small feeble joint in the car together—as much of your age-old stash as you could scrape out of the baggie bottom. You're reduced to this, a pathetic call to arms; she's in your arms and you are in hers with your legs crossed over, both wearing denim. You've both given a great confession into the windshield. (I love my family and can't really see, what? Giving that up. I mean, well, I'm not sure what I mean except I can't see it, the cost is too high, not high enough, higher than I thought it would be, maybe, maybe exorbitant, or I'm a wimp, scared, too feeble to go for it, unwilling to shake up the world, maybe, maybe not, or else we're just not right enough.) Your combined breath has fogged the glass all the way across except for two dimples of clarity where the vents are pumping hot air, and through these you can just make out the wooden railing, and past that the sea dark black catching the first quivers of the rising moon. You confess your love for your kids. For your respective partners. For the universe beyond the sea. For the moon in the dense darkness. For the Cape. For the land. For this spot. For the flaccid odors of the pine swamp. For the things you see. For the things you'll never see. Up in the dune grass a stone marker stands on the spot where the pilgrims first came into hostile contact with the Indians. You admit that you're saving that. You're going to use it in a short story. Smoke drifts, you hold it, gasping for air, gasping and then choking and lunging a laugh out. Passing the joint her way, holding the flame over the remnants, a pinkie nail–sized fleck of rolling paper. There is a lightness in your chest just under the ribs.

—Didn't fuckin' Abraham have to sacrifice his only son, or at least begin to, I mean he was like just about to knife his own kid's throat and all that but he didn't.

—He didn't, she says. He didn't. And she opens the door and steps into the cold and walks along to the railing, and you see her but hold off on running after her mainly for reasons of drama; to run to her would be unseemly, and there is more dramatic element in letting her stand out there a moment (and you realize of course how much the dramatic element has played a role in all this, and how young and stupid you sound, stoned, like your own sons).

Y) Pressing the iron into the wrinkled blouse, wedging the bow around, a ship working across the sea—you think fleetingly of his tongue.

Z) In the winter, the waves rearrange the landscape into seasonal formations—beaches grow short and stout. You watch a time-lapse film at the National Seashore visitor's center. You came here on the way back from the beach just to warm up. The dated film clatters away—shifting sands, a flex and wane of the days jolting past one after another with great rapidity. Something about the time lapse. The music swells—you've seen the movie before—and the view expands as a helicopter shot pans back and slowly reveals the Cape itself hooking out feeble and deprived like the quivering, wanting hand of a drug addict longing for the needle. You're lonely seeing it, those spots of wanton love and lust. The lights go on and you clutch Irene's hand. She doesn't know a thing. The elements are stable and calm. Nothing has shifted. The boys are already out in the tourist information area. They're stealing maps again. One distracts the attention of the ranger with a stupid question and the other grabs a whole batch; it's the thing they do—these kids—stealing maps of all kinds, in large numbers, to be distributed one way or another to the rest of the world. There is no reason in it, but they're your kids. You don't support the theft part, but the random stupidity of their teenage desires you support wholeheartedly.

DUSTMAN
APPEARANCES TO DATE

Leaning into the wind, holding his hat, headlong toward the shed, with the billowing dust forming a squall line to his left, he seemed bent over before the immensity of his situation—the split-rail fence, the chicken wire, the barbed wire, the rugged boards of the stockade—yet at the same time he seemed resolved to be singular and hopeful. One imagines he got to the shed and harnessed the anxious horses and rubbed the sides of their heads and spoke to them while the sand seeped in the cracks and knotholes and the granular hiss sang against the boards. He'll persevere, live on, and make it work, or not work. The foreclosure papers might be served. Later he'll be seen swaying over the Oklahoma landscape when the wind is right, part dust dervish, and part dust devil, a composition of wheat chaff, dirt, and bits of road litter cohering into something that might catch your eye. His story began to spread. You see the dustman again t'day, Earl? Spot you another one of them dustmen? Nope, can't say I did.

∴

Most know that Crazy Horse spotted a dustman when he was wandering around shortly after Black Buffalo Woman ran off and got married to No Water. He fingered the good-luck stone behind his ear and worked his sickly horse to a gallop, but he couldn't catch the dustman. It moved ahead of him like the moon. It was a dustman of prophecy, dreamlike, with pantaloons that swirled around his legs, granules of dust that took on the dark bluish grays of a tornado cloud (Crazy Horse had seen his share of twisters); for a moment the dust-man paused, turned, and they had a silent conversation re-garding the nature of the horizon, lament for the coming warfare, and the demands inherent in the wind itself.

∴

Along the beach near Truro, Massachusetts, on August 1, 1889, a couple spotted a dustman rising from windblown sand and lime, remnants of clamshell and marl light enough to become airborne. He took the shape of the well-known pirate Sam Bellamy, whose treasure would eventually be found close to shore, in absurdly shallow waters. With hat astride his boney skull, whipping along the edge of the water, this dust-man seemed determined to reach the couple, who were run-ning away, craning their necks in what was called (in the

Provincetown *Gazette*) "an effort to make haste away from the creature, said dustman gaining on their running, said dust devil making his perambulatory, ethery way toward them until he came forward and broke away in a twirl of sand." He didn't speak, this dustman, but gestured as if he wanted to speak. Many creatures arising out of the swirling of dried bone and ash and vapory elements try to speak, one account concluded. They made hand gestures similar to those Native Americans used to communicate during times of warfare or hunting.

∴

During the huge mill fire near Nekoosa, Wisconsin, two heat devils tore loose from the fire—the combustion of five tons of notebook paper, a hundred tons of finished Christmas wrapping, along with twenty tons of tissue paper and fifteen tons of onionskin. (The carbon paper mill—two miles downstream—would suffer a similar fate a few years later. Both fires lit up the night sky for a hundred miles.) Two heat devils broke away from the inferno and, according to the fireman who witnessed the event, took dustman forms. One resembled Ben Franklin. The other was Thomas Paine, but the fireman couldn't put a name to the face. (By the way, Ben Franklin was a big believer in dustmen.) At that point the wind shifted and the fireman had to run from the heat. When he turned for one last look, the Ben Franklin dustman was making gestures, upward movements of his hands, as if conducting some ill-tuned, furious symphony. Similar figures were seen rising out of a tire fire in Northridge, Alabama, where a half million tires burned for weeks, producing a spume of dark oily smoke visible from the orbiting space shuttle. One astronaut claimed the cloud of smoke looked like Mickey Rooney; another noted a strong resemblance to Mickey Mantle. The owner of the tire pile—a guy named Albert Wayward—saw a face form in the commotion of heat and smoke. It was his father's face. It made a few halfhearted lip movements, attempted to speak, and then broke apart in the hot winds. Yeah, yes sir, yes indeed, it was Dad as sure as sure, he said. Pop was a miner. When I saw him it looked as if he were right out of the mine, covered with the dust. Even his teeth, for Christ's sake. Even his teeth were covered with coal dust.

∴

Most who witnessed the Devils Tower dustman were Lakota, who upon seeing him moved between two paradoxical modes: a reverent desire to bow down before the dust soul in honor, and a shoulder shrug at his inept attempts at communication. He lifted his arms above his head and spun around. He tried to move his lips. The dustman just couldn't get his words out. And this in the time of the ghost dance! A time of desperation! Of urgent calling upon the spirits! Spectacularly, the Devils Tower dustman lived for twenty long minutes (white-man time), working the currents that just happened—for those few moments in the random, wildly unkempt history of wind—to unite around those huge hunks of rock at the base of the tower into a conveyor belt of air that swooped him back and forth along a span of about a quarter

mile; during this swooping, he transmogrified from an uniden-
tifiable face to that of General George Armstrong Custer. The
Custer dustman grimaced in pain. A fine powdery dust gave
luster to his long hair (and nixed the idea that this appearance
foretold the battle at Little Bighorn. For that battle, Custer had
his hair cropped close to the skull). The Devils Tower dustman
dematerialized in a dramatic fashion. Instead of widening into
a gyre of dust—as was the standard terminal mode of most
dustmen—this one spun into a tight whip visible only as a
small fissure in the atmosphere, a slice in the horizon, snapping
off to the east.

∴

Fulvous dust bowl dust mixed with Portland cement dust
and limestone dust along with bits of street dust composed
the only distinctly urbane dustman appearance (recorded),
swirling up Thirty-second Street past the recently completed
Empire State Building, bounding down the street aloft on the
combined city currents that tore east-west across Manhattan.
Some say the oblong cranium formed a keen resemblance to
F. Scott Fitzgerald. Although one recent arrival to the city
(from the west) identified the dustman as Rexford Tugwell,
head of the Resettlement Administration, others saw nothing
but a big billowing cloud that quickly clenched into a goatlike
figure that hopped and leaped all the way to Hell's Kitchen before exploding.

∴

Only a select few witnessed the atomic dustman, rising from the Marshall Islands just after the mushroom spread into the heavens, shortly after the duck-and-cover of the first shock wave, as they stared through carbonized glass straight into the eyeball of the inferno, to see him there, resting softly, a grimacing flesh-skull caught in a paroxysm of fire—a face distraught but attuned to his own suffering. Some claimed he had an Einsteinian wildness, a crop of unkempt hair that spread up into the sky before fading into the tremendous nonsense of the smoke and fire. Those who admitted to seeing a face in the cloud wrapped their admission in tones of jest, chalking the atomic dustman up as just one more of those strange nuclear-blast phenomena: nuclear heat sprites, fire curls, and of course the infamous bandy-eyed lady who is known to impress herself on the inside of eyelids of atomic witnesses, belly dancing and twisting to some tight bongo beat. (If they had looked closely they would have seen the atomic dustman working his slack jaw over what seemed to be the word *geshem.*)

∴

The Nixon dustman appeared one Sunday afternoon (August 10, 1968) in the desert near Las Vegas. The huge benumbed skull of the Leader of the Free World was born out of a wicked squall, a rolling lip of grit similar to the great dust bowl kickoff storm in May of 1934, the one that blew "Kansas dirt" three hundred miles off the Atlantic coast and powdered the decks of so many ships. The '68 storm came out of the blue (literally) and produced the Nixon Dust Phenomena, as it came to be known: a Mt. Rushmorish, chiseled dustman that swooped down on two hippies who were not quite sure if what they were witnessing was a freakish aberration of nature or just some aftermath of a previous acid trip in which they'd seen dust figures—men and dogs, mainly—arise out of the turbulent sands of the desert. The Nixon dustman had the same smile/grimace that would appear on his face when he appeared publicly one last time, raising his arms skyward in a final so-long salute from the hatch of the presidential helicopter.

∴

Then, of course, the Hemingway dustman appeared near Cabo de Gato National Park. The dustman was sighted by an old peasant holdout dating back to the time of Franco, leading a donkey across the terraced, useless land, and a writer who summered in a house along the cliffs, who was having his afternoon martini on the back patio and happened to be looking east when a dust cloud rose up—as it had so many times before—out of the brisk afternoon winds. He studied the cloud's progress. That's a hell of a big dust cloud, he thought. It's clearly larger than the usual dust clouds. It looks as though a man's face is appearing. Yes, there's a skull shape. And lips. And brows. And a forehead. Holy Christ, that's formidable beard growth. Meanwhile, down in the *rambla*, the peasant shouted in recognition. The Hemingway dustman outlived all other dustmen, almost outperforming the Grand Tetons dust ghost, a cloud sighted by campers one afternoon that took the shape of a great bear and lasted for at least an hour, a great humping beast of tree smoke (forest fire) and golden pine pollen.* As if fueled by the great myth of the man himself, the accidents and broken bones, the falls and plane crashes, the Hemingway dustman backtracked and flew once again over the writer's house before launching himself out over the Mediterranean, where he sucked water into a pale blue skirt, as if to mock the dry, unyielding terra firma, a land that once nourished fine tomatoes—similar to those now produced by the drip-method farms fifty kilometers to the west, near Málaga.

∴

The Gogol dustman was sighted near St. Petersburg by a computer programmer named Gregor Petrovitch, as he was driving to his office. It formed out of dry summer air (there wasn't a lot of dust around), a clearly delineated face, and most certainly the face of Gogol, the same small neatly trimmed mustache, the long, dark hair parted on the far right, hanging limp to the side of his wide brow, the eyes soft above an abundantly long, fine nose. Petrovitch pulled over to the shoulder, got out of his car, and snapped a photo (he was an avid amateur photographer). It was the nose, for God's sake, he told the press. The nose was a dead giveaway. The nose grew until it dwarfed the head. A huge schnoz dancing over the countryside until it gave in to the whims of chaos and unfurled

* Bear dust ghosts in no way count as dustmen. Dustmen are a rare phenomenon, whereas dust animals and dust figures are spotted daily during the dry seasons, more often than not taking the form of pigs, pug-nosed animals, and, frequently, goats.

like a giant overcoat. It became known as the Dust Schnoz, the Dancing Nose, and then, later, when the photograph of the dustman was officially identified as Gogol, it was (officially) dubbed the great Gogol dustman, an abhorrent quirk of nature, a glorious case study in the physiognomy of the miraculous.

∴

Here one should make one final note about the archaeological theory—often cited in historical studies of Christ—that a great dust Christ was spotted near the Galilean town of Capernaum by shepherds, who shrugged the Christ dustman off as yet another one of many such aberrations, even, some say, as a mild annoyance.

[CARNIE]

The carnie rose slowly, a ragged display that no one seemed to notice until it was completely up; at least his daughter didn't notice it until, passing on the way home from school (John picked her up most days when he was working the night shift, buying and selling power for the local utility), she spotted the Ferris wheel and begged him to take her, to let her go. You'd have thought it was the first time she'd seen a Ferris wheel, the way she went on about it, he told his wife later. Carnivals were risky affairs, with their inept machinery, assembled in haste, and above all the hawkers and roadies, halfwits and assorted drunks, riffraff who had traveled to the ends of the earth and were the worse for wear. He saw them come through town when he was growing up in Illinois: souls lost to the tedium of taking tickets and standing hours in the hot sun helping people on and off rides. Deep inside (it is safe to say) John had a healthy respect for them, a high regard for the extremes that roadies were seemingly able to put up with. He loved the dusty, half-mown fields where they usually set up, the way late-afternoon light drove through the tangle of equipment.

But his respect wasn't enough to put his fears aside.

∴

Consider Ned Alger. Ned manned one of two machines, depending on what his partner, Zip Jones, felt like working; if Zip was running the merry-go-round, Ned would take his shift at the Romper ride, a wide spider of metal fatigue flinging kids in sloppy circles. None of the rides worked at full speed. If you were to look, you'd see Ned standing with an absent, empty look on his face watching the machine run; you'd see his nervous tic of crossing his arms over each other, up high across his chest, and heaving great bellows of air in and out, as if he'd just lifted himself from an exhausting swim. He suffered from the cigarette dangling off his lips. If you were to spend a day watching the two of them go from one machine to the other—silently changing places with an unspoken commitment to breaking up the tedium—you'd wonder, What currents exactly kept Zip and Ned together? What bonds—sacred and otherwise—held them fast? Truth was, they were linked simply by their point of departure: both joined the carnie when it was passing through a small town in Ohio. Zip was hitching aimlessly from the west and needed some cash. Ned, who was living in the town at the time, saw a help-wanted flyer in a Laundromat and decided it was his chance to see the world.

More than that, though: the long-simmering nothingness of the fields beyond the edges of the towns in which they set up; bluegrass and timothy and planted hay and corn dried to a brittle song; the endless, almost needless horizon. They came from that, both men, two years of passing town to town.

The kid was begging and he agreed to take her. Simple as that. Later, he had to see it that way.

∴

Zip was halfway through a bottle of gin. The workday was done and most of the roadies were lounging about the campers, smoking, mulling. A bit of corn had lodged between his front teeth, and he was working his tongue against them, taking pleasure in the effort, unwilling to use his fingers except as a last resort. He'd made a kind of testimony to himself this evening—working at the corn—about some things he had done a few towns back, in Pennsylvania; *some things* was how he thought of them, although if he wanted he could conjure up exact memories: break-ins of houses in the afternoons when most suburban folk were off earning their two-income keep, jimmying a door or kicking in a basement window and lowering himself into the damp, cobwebbed basement of some sodbuster's estate. In Ohio—two years ago—he copped a couple of off-the-cuff fondles in the bushes; he could remember the wet mouth beneath his palm as he pushed hard to smother the words trying to come out. Working at the corn in his own mouth he began to speak to himself—as he often did—in his own manner: a few tidbits of biblical cadence and phraseology—thou arts, therefores—blended in with what the other guys called Zip-speak, because he had his own particular way of talking.

Don't know likely what the bejesus you'd be doing to be doing what you are is a good example. Or: *Fuck that fuck I'm gonna fuck him until he wishes he were fucked.*

Now he held his head back, way back, and let a little moan slide from his gullet. The gin was settled into the base of his gut, not enough to warm him but enough to make more necessary.

∴

Yeah, there are myths about this kind of thing, and one wants to avoid stereotypes—plenty of good folk working the road even to this day, the very beginning of the century, anachronistic as hell but there, smoking, trying to work out the general situation. So be it. This is his story. This is what happened in this particular incident.

It was the other one, Ned, who did the real wandering. Late at night when all was shut down and the dormant machines stretched their weary metal joints (you could hear them sigh in the wind), he might steal off for a walk, a journey, a venture, a poke around town, working his way stealthily through fence gaps and along the backsides of hedges, toeing his way through the night-blue shadows. His travels took him along the topologies of night: garbage cans resting silently on the curb, awaiting pickup; toys left outside to gather shawls of dew; stray dogs and cats slinking on their betrayed hind legs. He walked through expensive backyards with gas grills and swimming pools and elaborate alarm systems and sensors that he was able to evade, except for once, in Canton, Ohio, when a loud siren went off and lights came on and he was chased like a fugitive (as he told it later, to Zip), like Harrison Ford in the movie—caught and put in the tank overnight with nothing to prove he'd actually done anything. His radar was off that night, he thought, he wasn't paying his usual attention— because if there was one thing he did do, and knew he did, it was to mind, to pay heed to what was before him; it was his Indian shit, he told Zip, not getting into the details—that he'd been raised by a squaw, his old lady, old-school Indian stuff, a real squatter who'd crammed his soul with so much junk he could hardly stand to feel it there; he was a tiptoer; he'd seen it growing up—men able to find ways into the darkness, to tread lightly.

∴

One would like to know exactly what it was that filled Ned when he walked through yards and places unspoken for by the light; perhaps it was the way he felt growing up, in the little squat in Petoskey, a patch of land they'd claimed as their own by parking the old bullet-shaped

Airstreams side by side. Behind them sat the chief's yellow Winnebago. And behind that, almost hidden in the wind blind of pines, stood the two teepees, trying to make it legitimate.

∴

You see, there are varieties of darkness. It's as simple as that. All day pitching the ride and smoking and looking up into the hard, ungiving eye of the sun while kids got on the Romper and rested their little rumps to be flung up and down. The eyes of the parents glimmered with their love, big, wide love, because what else would compel them to buy three fifty-cent tickets for a measly five minutes of being spun around on old rusted equipment? Neon bulbs worn out to a damp glow; music, once supplied by a real, air-piped organ, now the same crappy tunes came from the Sony boom box he propped in the center of the merry-go-round. Every thirty minutes he had to go turn the tape over.

∴

There are fears so deep and dark that to admit them is to feel the universe slip out from under your own feet; or so John thought. If touched upon too long, these fears would flower out over your skin—the very skin of your life—like a huge wart. He'd seen photographs in a porn magazine of untreated growths flowering like mushrooms from the skin. Guys in the break room were passing it around, and he sat in stunned submission to what he was seeing: a giant, cauliflower growth in the crack of a man's ass. To think that it could go like that untreated. He stared so hard and long at the photo that finally Rick, who had bought the magazine and felt it was his to stare at long and hard like that, took it back. The next Sunday he went to church and spoke to God in the hopes of never having to face any such thing in his own life. He wasn't asking for protection; his hope was that God would forget him, pass him over, allow him to walk through his life untouched.

When, in retrospect, he saw the man on the merry-go-round stumble back to change the cassette; when he saw the man then move back to hold on to the pole directly behind his daughter; when he saw the way the man was looking at his daughter, and the droop of the faded Wranglers; when he thought back and retraced everything, he was sure he should have *seen it*: there were wide-open empty spots all over the ride. The first swellings of a skin growth, and he should have spotted it.

∴

One theory might be that carnivals provide a natural outlet for a darker need we all have to play ourselves against the forces of transience; a neatly polished road show would go against that need. Dejects, freaks, wash-aways run the rides. The state inspector—half blind with foggy cataracts—comes in for a show of civilized examination. He holds his clipboard and checks the joints of the Ferris wheel, and maybe watches the men work lug nuts onto bolts. But he avoids inspecting the undersides of the men's souls.

Strangely enough, the paths of John and Ned had crossed before, on a beach in northern Michigan, near the encampment in which Ned grew up. (No one was really sure how he got the name Ned, or even Alger, his mother calling him Alger but also the Indian name of Walk Moon, too; and there was the man who was supposed to be standing in as his father, Jack-somebody, who came in at night with his belt already undone.) Two women sat on the beach in Petoskey State Park, at the cusp of Little Traverse Bay. It was an unusually cool midsummer day and the beach was almost empty—both women sat watching their sons play, far up, near the waterline. Of course John didn't remember that day, amid countless other days going to the Midwest to visit his grandparents at their summer cottage, but he did remember the ragtag encampment of residual beings where Ned was reared, and the warnings his grandfather had given him to stay away from the camp. A shaggy little creek wove through the myrtle along the side of the road there, loaded with broken gin bottles and potato chip bags, and through the weeds one could see the old trailers, and men and women in lawn chairs drinking beer.

∴

The idea of blind chance put a hole in John's gut; he refused it outright as an available explanation. It just wouldn't do. John made a vow that he would never admit in any way that the *whole* thing hinged on brutal good luck (from Ned's vantage) and bad luck (from his vantage) and nothing else. The fact that his daughter had been at the carnival that day and taken a twirl (sixteen rotations) on Ned's ride allowed him to make the connection between the two that led to a legal conviction; but that was all. When he tried to visualize it he came up with the image of a huge arc, a bolt of raw, blue charge going from his house to that ride. A bolt fired by fate, by forces begun by his own actions. After wandering around, Ned found himself beneath her window, hunched in the thickness of the hydrangea bush, eying the partway-open window and getting his X-Acto knife out to slice through the nylon screening with only the faintest of zips, the blade easing through the squares the way a very hot scoop curled back ice cream. Then with both hands spread out, he lay his palms on the underside of the window and lifted it slowly (the window grooves had been recently waxed to reduce friction, which caused brain-deadening lead dust), softly enough so the sound of it was actually nothing more or less than the usual movements of night: trees rasping each other in the gentle upheaval of breeze, or a raccoon scuffing the side of an overturned garbage can. He lifted himself acrobatically into the window— his footfalls on landing softened, he felt, or dreamed, by all of history, his imagined forefathers tiptoeing the wooded trails along the shore of Lake Huron.

Jesus expelled the demons from the freaks and then sent the fuckers into a herd of swine and drove them headlong over a cliff, John read a year later, trying to find his way into some kind of answer, attending a Bible study at the local evangelical church, reading the passage and then saying fuck this and getting up and walking out to the back of the building where kiddie swings made movements in the wind. He heard the soft squeals of the pigs in the air as they made lopsided motions over the edge, the thuds as they hit the ground. He read somewhere else, too, that driving out the demons only leaves a large, vacant recess into which more evil slips.

∴

You see, to tell it as a story or even a series of actions would be to make sense of it and to lend it some kind of orderly function in the world; that's why it is only referred to by the media as the incident—the girl's name, of course, withheld to protect her future; and her muteness, her silence, around the event was part of that withholding; in the horrifying darkness Ned went in and *did what he did*, and it was the basics that held sway in the public mind: the entering of the dark room, the violation of the safe, almost sacred silence of night, the pink ruffle curtains and the canopy bed.

∴

Zip sensed right away that Ned had gone and *done it* again, something mighty bad. Dawn was pink along the horizon. A brush of high ice clouds licked the sky. Both men hunched beneath blankets, unwilling to leave the herringbone, slip-proof surface of their beloved merry-go-round. They heard the tink, tink of metal adjusting to the cold and, when the wind rose, a rattling of the Ferris wheel guy wires. Might as well be any place on earth as being in this town, Zip said softly. The talk was like that, soft, with a fibrous quality. Smell somethin' bad coming in this air, Ned, he said. Off far in the trees, like a bit of lint in a comb, there was the sound of the sirens—the rescue crews and cops, all the attendant caregivers coming to open the girl up with their interviews. He knew it would take them a while to pry out the story from her scared soul—if the truth were told, he had, for a small second, a flick of remorse for the other side of the world (as he thought about it): the dark brooding spirits that his grandmother used to mutter about through her leathery lips—there is a darkness in the whiteness of that world that I shouldn't bother with if I were you, boy. You're a fucking Indian squat, nothing more, and don't forget it. So he got his rucksack from the trailer, stuffed it as quickly as he could, gave Zip a kiss on the mouth, and went off to find the interstate, where if he was lucky he might catch a hitch someplace else. He'd change his name and identity, find a new way of showing himself to the world, and then hook back up with the carnie the way he had before, just shaving off his beard and getting his hair cut short in the back and then going right up to Nate and asking for work (Nathan would know damn well that it was Ned with another name and face). The carnie was heading west, he knew, and would hit a few pathetic state fairs as sideshow backup and then a few Ohio town festivals before the tremendously boring hinterland towns of Indiana (that's where he would finally reunite with his beloved Zip).

∴

Working backward, John went over the events of that day and made diagrams, flowcharts resembling those intricate schematics of computer innards. He examined the whole day from the very start, when he woke her up, nudged her softly, and gave her breakfast of frozen waffles, one thing leading to another, which led eventually to that ride. (Ned had been captured, finally, in Albany, after an APB went out on him over fax machines. Irrefutable proof in the form of hair samples found on her sheets and in Ned's trailer linked the crime to the carnie.) A crew of jaded cops and medics and social workers hung around long after the event to give some assurance to the family that they were doing all they could in every way. It was no use. Behind him John felt the web of events untangled, like an old used-up fishing net washed ashore. It was all there, in the past, gone, lost. Nothing would ever change it. And yet he felt it might be changed. He pondered it for a year, for another year, for the rest of his life. He lived simply outside the world of rational thought. He kept his toes in the magic. He pondered the electric spark and went on with his life; he even, a few years later, took her to another carnie as a way of going through the pain (as was suggested by the social workers).

∴

The carnie went on to Indiana, to Laketon, where it set up for another firemen's fund-raiser. With rheumy eyes, the crew got the rides up during an afternoon that was as dry and hard as peanut brittle, heaving parts from the flatbed, working slowly with a bored somnolence, hammering with wooden mallets, making what used to be music to a kid's ear but now went unheard mostly behind car windows. The edge of the town simmered with insects. To the left of the lot there was nothing but a flat field that married the horizon; to the right of them was the last house in town, in which an old man lived alone. Staring at it, Zip could tell an old fart lived there, what with the weathered clapboards and the rusting tools on the wooden bench out back. Indeed, the old man came out, unfolded a lawn chair, took a pipe and wedged it into his teeth. He watched them for hours on end with a blank expression. There, Zip thought. I was right. An old codger working his way through the last of his days. His visions were coming more often since Ned had been caught, and his Zip-speak was even stranger, more fanatic, mostly incomprehensible babble to the other roadies, who avoided him completely if they could. *You can't Christ-all this fucking nothingness*, he said. *He's going to hell-fuck 'fore I get to fuck him myself*. Some even admitted they were scared of the Zip. For a moment, resting his back against a canopy support beam of the merry-go-round, which he was assembling by himself (there were a few bolts missing), he had one of his visions again—the old man with a blade between his eyes, lodged deep. In honor of Ned, I just might make this one vision come to pass, he said aloud. Then he shook the thought off the way you'd shake away an ice cream headache. The carnie was going up piecemeal. A real half-assed job. It would be inspected by a bribed official of the state, who just happened to be passing through the town to visit his great-aunt. It would have the usually dusty lightbulbs strung from a feeble infrastructure, and the people would arrive sensing the dubiousness of the whole affair, as if it were nothing but a holding pen for castoffs. That's what they liked about it, essentially. It gave them a sense of being ripped off, betrayed, denied. They hated it but loved it. Hordes came through the gate on opening night. Stayed a few hours. Left glad to leave. It was Zip who got to stay, alone with his bottle, sprawled back on the cold plate steel, watching the old man's house, shrouded in darkness, stark against the dark horizon like a cardboard prop. It wasn't real enough. It stood as a testament to the unreality of the world.

[THE NEST]

The storm window didn't fit properly in the grooves, and somehow a queen got in and built her first few cells and then the workers matured and they constructed additional units until, clumped in the left-hand corner, facing east toward the Atlantic, with a perfect symmetry, a round nest appeared. They were working vigorously when he discovered them one afternoon, shortly after his arrival at the summerhouse. Hovering at the top of the window, they exited through the gap to forage the yard. The window shade kept the nest hidden for several days, but eventually—cleaning the windows— he rolled it all the way up, saw the nest, became enamored, and began studying it carefully. Now he feels an obligation to terminate the hive. To scrutinize it for another day—no matter what kind of intrigue and entertainment it might provide—

would appear obsessive. The normal act of looking at the habits of the wasps as they go about their business, using his scientific background as an excuse for close study, the fact that he has always been interested in entomology, along with etiology, is beginning to look demented, he thinks, standing at the window, feeling his fingers twitch. As a surgeon, he has often pondered his fingers and their value to his practice—a lucrative orthopedic partnership focusing on the hands of highly paid athletes and musicians, along with a large share of standard knuckle jobs (he's the master of the artificial joint), congenital abnormalities, and carpal tunnel fix-ups. His leave of absence was sparked by two major factors: (1) after eighteen years of marriage, his wife left him for another man, a young entertainment attorney named Richard Clayton; and (2) suddenly, he grew tired of staring into the beauty of the opened flesh, visceral, bright against the pale blue surgical drape, while the sound of his own breath behind his blood shield—once slightly romantic, soft, and alluring—had become annoying, a reminder of his own bodily functions and the simple stupidity of involuntary functions.

∴

At the window, he stands looking at the nest, trying to ignore the hip-hop beat coming from downstairs, knowing that Andrea is watching videos against his wishes and that he should go down and confront her, but also feeling unable to do so, actually afraid to do so, because to make her stop watching would be to deny her yet another delight. And now, without her mother, all she has—aside from whatever love he can give—is delights in the form of her friends at sea camp, sea camp itself, ice cream (trips nightly to the premium ice cream outlet, or the cheaper frozen custard stand), and television. In the last two weeks she has become not only more assured in her manner but also, strangely, lighter, wispy in her uncaring attitude. Her arguments seem to shoot up from a great depth, surfacing at strange angles that have nothing to do with the issue at hand, he thinks, staring into the darkness. So if I did go down and speak to her, she would sit, shrug, snap off the set, and not say a word until, later, asking her to brush her teeth, she'd scream: You're always telling me what to do, you're always treating me like a little kid. I'm not a little kid anymore.

∴

He continues to observe the nest while outside the dusk thickens around the pine trees, three of them, and the single sugar maple that roots itself in the soft, sandy soil, surrounded by a sea of poison ivy. From the nest there is the glint—some gold, more silver—of quivering wings. The nest is a dark brood of shadow in the upper corner, but he can visualize their formation, huddled against each other—maybe for warmth, although it's still warm outside. The sky is clear, speckled with stars, and it will get cooler in a few hours when, as usual, he comes back to examine them again, before he tries to go to sleep. They'll be still, shivering slightly, their feelers probing, testing, aware, alert in their slumber. He'll feel the oddness of his observational pattern. This is the second night he's come to the window—with Andrea supine on her bed, wrapped in milky-white sheets—to look them over one last time before he goes to bed. In the afternoon he came up to examine the nest, watching as they entered and exited through the crack, positioning themselves on the flange of aluminum before launching out into the haze over the yard, dropping slightly before striking out with precision, as if they knew exactly where to go.

∴

And maybe they did. There was a persistence to the way they came and went. In the summer heat the nest was half full, or half empty. The lucky ones returned with bits of food, green leaf parts, and even, in one case, an offering of a spider—which the workers chewed vigorously and shoved into the cells. (In the cells the larvae could be seen wiggling softly.) That afternoon the nest served to remind him of their last time together, as a family, when he and Lydia had attended the Hook Mountain Elementary School spring concert and heard Andrea playing her flute with the band. A morass of notes, most off-key, somehow cohered into a song called "Hot Cross Buns." Mr. Frank, the band director, was pounding his baton up and down so vigorously that it was clear he did so to keep the audience's attention on him and away from the atrociousness of the band. But now he's feeling odd about his reaction to the nest. He leans close to the glass and whispers to them: O ye who find within the brain stem the semblance of orderly existence! O ye who shall inherit the earth. O ye brutally adaptive creatures!

∴

Certainly he has been deprived of sleep, not only because of tensions caused by the pending divorce but also by the noise of his daughter's breathing, which was caused by sleep apnea, by large adenoids—most likely—that were creating a disturbance in her breathing patterns, deep silent moments when the breath ceased before her involuntary systems kicked in and she took great sucking gasps of air that woke him up— if he was lucky enough to be asleep. His friend Jenks had made the diagnosis and stated that she had probably been suffering for a few years. —You're just noticing this now, Russ, because you're up at night and aware of her breathing. And no, I don't think this has anything at all to do with family tensions. It's not a psychosomatic reaction of any kind.

∴

He watches them in the morning after Andrea has left for camp, sipping his coffee, examining their activities, speaking to himself. O ye who have no weight on the world. O ye who can survive the simple redundant tasks! O ye who perform with precise grace! Touching his fingers to his lips. In the afternoon the heat is relentless, thick. The sun sits in the sky with acetylene brilliance, chalky and pure. The nest, he thinks, is a frightening soothsayer. Andrea is afraid of bees,

wasps, and the smaller flying insects. Not so much a phobia—
because certainly she goes to sea camp, and he assumes that she
confronts insects there, in the fields, where they shoot archery
in the morning before they go out to sail, sending arrows into
round pads stuffed with hay. (Dad, even your own heartbeat
can interfere with your shot; even your heart can mess you up,
Dad, she said.) But she has a skittish fear of flying insects. He
and Lydia used to trace the fear back to a moment in Spain.
Locating the origin of her fear had seemed an act of deep love;
the impossibility of parental detective work made it fun and
infinitely complex. The original sting took place about thirty
miles from Mojacar, in a small village in the Costa Blanca.
Their house was up on a buff overlooking the Mediterranean.
It was evening and the light drew low across the rubble as they
followed the path along the road, past a few peripheral apartments, up around the switchbacks, to the flat mesa where the
house stood, windswept, recently whitewashed, stark white in
the fading light, surrounded by deep green vegetation. Up
there the wind sang through the guy wires of a shortwave
tower behind the patio. The villa was owned by a former patient, a retired Federal Reserve VP named Connors who had
suffered severe wrist problems, carpal tunnel complicated by
the early stages of arthritis. (It's from moving all that gold
around, he joked. The stuff is real. We're not GS but we still
have plenty of the heavy metal. Money is a weighty thing. I've
thought a lot about this and I'm sure you'll understand when
I say that much of my job was beyond my own comprehen-
sion.) Along the back of the house, the white stone driveway

was bordered with a flagstone wall. Each time they came home from the beach she mounted it and walked, stepping carefully. They stayed behind her, that evening, a few yards back, watching. The nest was in a crevice between two stones. This time, her foot hit the nest. The wasps stung the back of her neck—ah the pale, delicate skin! and the top of her feet—oh those tiny little feet! They held her and soothed her and explained that wasps weren't bad or nasty or anything and that they were really nice. Funny bees. Good bees, they said. Bees were softer and bumbly. Bees were just as surprised and maybe as scared as she was, even more so, perhaps. From the bee's vantage, you're a big giant girl. You're huge to the bees. Bees are scared of you. Scaredy-cat bees. They did everything they were supposed to do as good parents to make the situation clear, real, and understandable, and to shed light onto the complexities of the natural world, but she still cried too long and woke that night asking for help and, from that moment on, shied away from anything that moved like a stinging insect: flies, gnats, mosquitos, and even small birds. O ye sublime creatures, he whispers to the nest in the window. He wants to sing to them and examine them and shove his hand up there and touch. His fingers are long, elegant, beautiful. He looks at them, pressed against the glass. The wasps hardly notice. They glance, jitter a bit, but are much too busy to care because the day is heating up, and heat is their fuel, and they must move in exact correlation to the temperature. The sun lurks over the shed in the yard. The sun pounds against the dry grass. The trees jab the unmoving air. His fingers flatten against the window. The tips are longer than most. He likes to think there's some predestination in their form. Yet he knows this isn't true. Fate is like a reversible coat. Andrea's fear has given him the obligation of removing the nest before they bring nightmares into a sleep already disrupted by her large adenoids.

∴

Then, later that afternoon, after a short nap, he shoves his hand up into a wasp nest. The windows in the summerhouse are low to the floor, so he has to hunch down to get his arm up between the two panes of glass, and by the time he touches the nest—a wild fuzz of movement—he's been stung on the hand, along the length of his arm, and on his belly. Some possible reasons behind his actions might be:

(A) basic sadomasochistic tendencies/to inflict pain as a way into his soul;

(B) deeper sympathetic urgencies/to connect physically with the efficiencies of the nest;

(C) a Christian salvation paradigm/to use the pain to find a way into rebirth;

(D) direct correlation between his occasional failing as a surgeon and his desire to inflict acute pain on his right hand, his suturing hand (see A);

(E) a state of general exhaustion and boredom that brings him to attempt something stupid just for the hell of it, because he's been calculating and thinking about the fact that when he taps the glass there is a moment when most of them freeze like rabbits, and maybe he can get his hand up there and feel the nest before they bite; he's just sick of thinking about it and therefore does it.

He thinks, before he shoves his hand up: it is strange to be a man, alone in a summerhouse with my daughter, spending two whole days staring at a wasp nest, and maybe by taking the bull by the horns, so to speak, I can at least find the courage to destroy them with insecticide. He does feel something up there, a soft warmth from their bodies; the crisp, thin delicacy of the gray paper and, inside the cells, because he gets his fingers around the nest for a second, a soft nubile protean life-form. He yanks his hand back against the storm window, cracks the glass (a sharp crescent moon), and then pulls it down and out, swatting at the ones who have entered the room, groping for the top of the window, shoving it closed, still swatting, dancing, doing a jig around the carpet, trying to find some way past the sublime agony—pinpoint-sharp stings—and to avoid the one little bugger who seems to be coming back for the counterattack. He shuts the door to her bedroom and crosses the hall and balls himself on his bed, where, for a moment, he makes small grunting noises, high-pitched, strange, maniacal. If you were to happen upon this man, curled on the bed, you'd conclude that he was mad. His grunts are tight in the throat, growing higher in pitch. Spooning into himself, embracing his knees, making noises, heaving with agony, he'd remind you of those patients you saw at the Michigan mental hospital, haunted vestal figures of complete isolation and loneliness who because of some snap in brain function had been reduced to vestiges of so-called functioning humans. You'd think of them immediately, seeing him, and you'd say to yourself, This is one fucked-up man, in one strange situation, who has just reached up and attempted to grasp a wasp nest.

∴

Back when he was happily married to his wife, Lydia, the doctor was unloading the trunk of the car, which was parked under the low-hanging branches of the only maple in the yard, when he felt something brush his head. He was startled. Intuition told him to recoil. The hornet nest was a large one, built around a low branch—one of those swirling gyres, layers of delicate paper (like a croissant) flaking around an inner comb. The hornets emerged from a rictus at the center, and he was lucky, deeply lucky, he told Lydia, in the kitchen, holding her in his arms, that he wasn't stung. —I mean I just stood up from the trunk and here it was, the nest, for God's sake, right against my head. They went outside together and examined it and felt the chilly mystery of the industrious way the nest surrounded the leaves and the branch. Later, in the evening, he went out when things were quiet—when all the hornets had returned home—and sprayed insecticide into the nest. In the morning he knocked it down with a stick. The dead hornets peppered the white stones of the driveway. In pieces the nest looked small, feeble, caved in like a dead animal. A few of the larvae twisted slightly inside the comb. He sprayed them, too, just to be civil about it.

∴

Again he stands at his daughter's window observing the wasp nest, up in the corner, between the storm window and the casement, built there in the spring, when the house was shut tight and the queen found the space where the window refused to meet the groove—a flaw perhaps in the production of the frames—and, having built her single small central structure, in which her workers hatched, was now the proud owner of a large nest of tight-waisted yellow wasps. He's standing at the window reminiscing about a patient named Bartres, a pianist from Argentina who once reached across his desk during a preoperative conference and said: —You have wonderful hands, beautiful fingers—octave fingers—and I will entrust my entire career to all ten of them. Bartres was a prodigy who, on approaching his first keyboard at five, had pecked out the Beethoven "Pathetique" Sonata by ear. The pianist saw his own abilities as deeply mysterious, a gift handed over by fate and therefore subject to fate's whims. He was a nervous wreck who had to be nursed along carefully, given extensive explanations of the nature of rheumatoid

subluxations of the joints and shown each step of the procedure, the cracking open of the bone and the insertion of the
joints (at which point the doctor handed over one of the small,
round, glossy pebbles of Dycron that was to replace the natural joint and watched as Bartres rolled it between his thumb
and index finger). The procedure failed. There was a bad heal-
up. A few weeks later the patient was seated sullenly in the
chair across from his desk with his bandaged hands heavy in
his lap, eyes wet and empty as he mumbled a prayer. Gently
he told the pianist, just as he had told other patients, that a bad
heal-up was a gross error in the judgment of God. It was a
highly unprofessional statement. But it made sense to put a
spiritual spin on the fact that some joints never mend, and that,
in some patients, the Dycron pebbles sit uselessly amid the wet,
glossy tissues.

∴

He has just blasted a wasp nest with insecticide and is
standing at the window examining a single wasp that
somehow endured the ordeal; a single wasp he dubs the Lone
Survivor, standing astride the flange of the window (some
kind of factory defect in the way the window meets the frame,
he thinks), fiddling his leg in his jaw, cleaning himself judi-
ciously, seemingly ignorant of the plight of his fellows, who
are mostly dead, falling to the windowsill below or writhing
into themselves with a tremendous fury, performing twisty
dances, smearing themselves with Knockdown. Those who

weren't struck directly by the Knockdown flew wildly for a few seconds in the mist. He sends another blast into the nest and mutters: That should do it. Then he goes downstairs to re-fill his coffee mug and comes back up to find the Lone Survivor still poking around the top of the nest. For several days he has observed their habits and the way they organize themselves around the required tasks of keeping the hive alive, going out into the yard—it's been one hell of a hot summer—to forage for food, bringing back tidbits of stuff, bits of pro-tein food matter and leaves and even, in one case, a piece of something that looked very much like a potato chip. He's been up there for hours at a time, going only to use the bathroom or to eat or, in one case, to drive into town to pick up a few packets of shingles—relishing the butcher paper wrapping, the heavy feel of the tar slabs as he threw them down into the trunk—because from his vantage at her window he noticed that the shed across the yard, which he built for Lydia's gar-dening tools, needs to be reshingled. The wild intricacy of their work fascinates him; the solitude and silence of the nest, too, and the way there seems embedded in their frenzy, in the briskness of their movement during the apex of the hot after-noon, a deeper significance, turning the nest into a kind of mandala. At the window he tries to pin words to it. He's weary from lack of sleep and has already, a day ago, done something astonishingly strange, shoving his hand up there and trying to grab it and instead, of course, getting stung up and down his arm, and on his belly. He feels a sinking sensation in his chest.

He feels deprived of air. His rib bones are aching with a desire to weep. The Lone Survivor searches the yard—the high cirrus clouds sweeping in from the Atlantic. A milky sky holds a single gull swooping over the three pines and the maple. The maple is deep green and out of place, trying to stay firmly rooted in the soft soil, moated by poison ivy. The Lone Survivor is mulling the vista, jittering his wings tight to his beautiful thorax, his glistening black body, adorned with a single red stripe, quivering. A soft inland breeze has worked through the dune head. He flutters lightly, gives a twitch with his feelers, and then—while the doctor mutters, Please wait, hold it right there, don't move, my little friend, I have something to say to you—launches skillfully into the air, dipping slightly until he becomes just one more bit of fuzz lost in a sea of chaff, even as the doctor tries the best he can to keep an eye on it, saying softly to himself, I don't know what to do with all of this, and then hearing, down below, the crunch of gravel as the minibus from camp pulls up, the mutter of a diesel engine, and then the slap of the screen door downstairs as Andrea enters the kitchen.

∴

Eventually he'll go down into the kitchen and sit with her as she eats a cookie and sips her milk and describes her adventures at sea camp, using the new words she has learned, coming about, in irons, tacking, and talking about how she shot arrows into the hay targets—holding her breath for control—what it's like to unfurl a spinnaker (it's like, like this giant shell that explodes with the wind), and how, eventually, in a few days, they're going to be tested on their knowledge so that they can graduate to the sloop and take the larger boats out, with the counselors, of course, far into the sea, beyond sight of land. Listening attentively, he'll put his hand on her wrist, on the spot where she was stung two evenings ago, while he was barbecuing; dashing out into the yard, she was windmilling her arms and making evasive zigzag maneuvers between the pine trees, falling to the ground and clutching her wrist. He'll say to her, —You're better now, aren't you? and she'll nod and rub her fingers across the spot, and he'll imagine her on the bow of a training sloop, firm-footed and able to translate the heave of the boat into a sure stance, legs slightly apart. Years have passed since that walk on the wall in Spain. Years remove them from the love that once held them tight. Thinking this, he'll hold her wrist a beat too long and remember what it was like to be a surgeon on an aircraft carrier during peacetime, when the only real duty was to appear presentable in Naples, and he'll think of the little Alpine Sunbeam he bought for Lydia, and how she drove it down from Rome to meet him in port, and how he bribed the quartermaster to allow the car on board, hefting it up and over with the crane, lowering it safely into the hold. And she'll pull her hand away from his and say, —Dad, Dad, are you okay? You're acting weird, softly, in a deepening voice, and he'll ignore her and reach up and brush the stray bit of salt-stiff hair from her brow and clear her forehead just so he can look at it, and he'll see that exposure to the sun has deepened the freckles in her face, and that her eyes have taken on a deeper blue, with shards of white, and that they seem, at least for the moment, strikingly beautiful.

[MICHIGAN DEATH TRIP]

HIGHWAY

A narcoleptic fit of a road: two lanes stretching east from
South Haven, running past defunct blueberry farms, weather-
beaten homes. Always a couple named Judy and Jack, stoned
in the backseat, unaware, embracing softly until the moment
the car violates the meridian line and confronts a tractor
trailer, hauling crated cherries out of Traverse City. Then
there's an abundance of fruit and blood and sparks spread out
across the dark road.

GUY WIRES

Some kid we knew, taking daredevil jumps on the back trails
up in Muskegon, roaring turns, throwing fans of snow skyward—safe and sound until twilight fell and the edge of the

trees became ensconced in blue and the rest of the world was impossible to see, including the telephone pole guy wire, which decapitated swiftly, neatly, leaving his head floating in the air (or so we imagined), against the tree line. (We had to wonder how long his head contained and held thought, how long—if at all—those eyes captured the snowscape before the shade slid down.) These snowmobile beheadings were once-a-year deaths that came assuredly out of the shift of the seasons.

ICE

A van full of stoners doing bong hits and driving out onto Walloon Lake in late November, after the first freeze-up, when it is just too fun and unavoidably pleasurable not to enjoy the hardness of the ice—newly frozen, translucent, and prone to gun-shot adjustments—too tempting to drive the van out onto a location that, just a few short weeks ago, seemed burdened with liquidity, waves slapping the boat hulls. All the kids had been out there, dangling lines, the lake silty and murky, lily pads encroaching on the south end. These kids were acquainted with the depths as they unfolded beneath the boat. Each knew the oil barrel raft under which, listening to the soft patter of afternoon water, one could gaze into the yellow depths the way God might stare between the clouds. So it was natural to drive the van out into the center, where soon—in a week or so—ice fishing shacks would appear. Most natural to test the ice in the largest way possible, stoned and happy. Most natural until—near the center—a crack opened, engulfed the machine, and returned the upper world to silence.

UNDERDRESSED

A kid out cross-country skiing, humping the poles, digging in, throwing back a good kick—the hard blue wax tossing the powder, and the bone-bent curve tense and tight against the snow—then up a hillock, leaving the herringbone marks across a landscape bisected by the Penn Central tracks to Chicago but otherwise natural and scrubby and, in the summers, a favorite of local dirt bikers who weave their ruts into the hills. So he is very wet and tired when he slows and rests for a moment, his breath puffing out in the subzero air, feeling the chill resting against the sweat of his spine, entering his hips. When he moves on to keep warm, coming up over another hill and into a glen, he catches his ski on a stump, falls, twists his ankle, and feels a tight snap. He dies silently, falling into the impenetrable darkness and then the unwillful sleep, head down in the soft snow.

FISH

Four kids in the Krogers parking lot at one a.m., standing around in the lingering heat, launching (stolen) fluorescent light tubes into the air one at a time, watching them descend, end over end, exploding into blooms of glass dust. Then the sword fighting begins. One kid named Earl picks up a tube and dashes it against the fender of a car, owned by a kid named Stanley, who in turn gives Earl a hard kick in the ass, not a light playful nudge but a solid boot in the crotch, coming up between the legs, catching the scrotum with the toe. All drama and tragic flourish, to get kicked in the balls. He clutches himself, emits a long, low moan, and falls to the pavement. Meanwhile, alongside this action, another kid is shoving shopping carts into a cement pylon. Then he tips one over, climbs it, and begins stomping. All this is accompanied by the car radio. (Could be any metal band of that time, most likely local talent, Iggy Pop, or Ted Nugent.) Earl is hunched over, drooling silently. Then the shopping cart kid rights a cart and shoves it at a blue Impala, colorless in the nonspectral light, catching the front headlight. This in turn inspires the kid named Stanley to pick up another tube and go toward the shopping cart kid. (Remember, these guys are all good friends and only trying to orchestrate some way deeper into the boredom, uniquely Michigan in quality, and to serve themselves up a dose of testosterone to go with the speed they ingested. Earlier that evening they went on a rampage to the fish hatchery, dumped yellow cartons of rat poison into a holding tank, and waited for the fish to float to the top, which they did, turning wide-eyed, betrayed, on their sides until the top of the tank—in the soft gentle starlight—was a sequined quilt of dead scales.) So when the kid who owns the car (Stanley) goes at the kid who pushed the cart, it is not only with the determined manner of someone bent on vengeance, but also with the extra zest of a common bond, of selfsame love, of approaching yourself in the mirror. He gives his friend one hard, swift, wide, arching swing into his face with the tube, which breaks against a cheekbone and somehow opens up like a blade and cuts deep into his neck, down at an angle into his aorta, unleashing a spume of blood. So when the kid hits the pavement—with a soft, doughy thump—he has already lost a large amount of blood and is succumbing to death the way you might fall into a soft pillow after a laborious day in the paint booth at Fisher Body Plant, or minding the rollers at the Parchment paper mill, or attaching door handles at Checker Cab.

COMET TAIL

With an experimental flourish, Charlene tried everything: codeine/wine; Valium/mysterious little green pill that seemed too small to do much, like one of her grandmother's saccharin tablets. Then there were the tight little bennies she took in the Vacation Court Hotel up near Houghton, one of those old strip hotels with a neon sign H20 BED/CABLE TV. The oar boats, long and cold, waiting—the *Myron*, the *Keweenaw*, the *Pewabic*— with hulls flaking rust. Vacation Court was home to lumber- jack types, to men with grizzly chins and temperaments hewn between Duluth and the Soo Locks. The hotel bathroom was mildewed and dank, with stalactites of golden stain drooping from the tub spouts. She was copping from a kid named Earl, gaunt and wasted with a slight hump in his back and standard self-carved letters on his knuckles: JESUCHRIST. Through his toothy grin he insisted she was going to fucking love the pills, indeed, for certain, and that she'd never thank him enough for the high she was about to receive, holding out the glimmering bag between two tight fingers as inducement to pay up. And how could she fail? Not because she knew the stuff was any good, or trusted his words, but because the beautiful little comet bag defied her to say no. She had that last-ditch look, the skin tight around her jawbone, some of her teeth missing. She was at the end of a certain line and he was going to help her get to the end of another. So when he was gone and relinquished of his charge, and she was ingesting the pills, there was no one to bear witness when she gasped for air, spoke the word oh, thinking as she did so, consciously, I'm passing out, way, way out, I'm going down, down, I'm sinking, I'm exploring space, I'm going interstellar, I'm going under, I'm slipping away. She died before the witness of God, if there is a God, and the view of the harbor from the window—limp steely waves upon which an ore boat made good speed to the center of Superior. The sky had a hard, unyielding edge, a bright blue tinged around the edges, toward Canada, with a veil of white haze. In a few hours the cleaning lady would discover her body, an arm tossed back like a flamenco dancer, pale and bright against the beige bedspread, her mouth open in one last sigh, as if her breath were there, hovering, shapeless and formidable around some last utterance.

KALKASKA INTERLUDE

A waitress wearing the light green singlet uniform with the ruffled skirt and the little name tag that says LIBBY, reciting "How can I help you" by rote now, a small smile that hooks more on the right than the left, and the hip-cock, too, with the pad posed. It's a flapjack place, mainly older folks, with the mint toothpick dispenser near the register; the large windows out front open to the vantage of the old state road. She's taking a smoke back behind the green Dumpster on a clear day, exhaling with pursed lips the fine stream. She feels on these breaks a certain exhilaration, a lifting sensation that belies the hours of tedium and hard work behind and in front of her life. She draws the smoke and feels the sun on her cheeks and the sensation, momentary but strong, of being rooted in this time and place. She will take Monday off and go north, driving hellfire for fire to Houghton to get to John before he goes off to captain the ore boat *Pewabic*. He'll be gone for at least a month as the boat works its way up the St. Lawrence Seaway, down the coast through the Panama, and then back up to deposit a load of copper ore at a Mexican foundry.

HUNTER

He hikes his last mile in without thinking. In two days he shot only a few anemic deer, leaving them to rot or freeze, his conduct most certainly unsportsmanlike. He loves the sensation of unleashing a shot at the unsuspecting deer, quick-frozen in fear, just before it turns to leap away. Yet he is not coldhearted. His pocket warmer has run out of batteries. His feet are cold and numb. He has folded his orange safety vest and wrapped it around his waist. His name is James and he is by trade a plumber, but he only works the larger, industrial jobs, spending months on a project—mainly laying plastic pipe, swiping glue around the joints, inhaling with pleasure—and avoids the small, domestic jobs so that he can go out hunting for weeks at at time. He's up near Muskegon, in state forest land, on a cool, clear, beautiful winter morning with the smell of pine sap and the windbreak of the tree line fine against the gray winter dawn. He's in peace. He's in silence. So the shot that comes out of the woods behind him, from the rifle of a kid just learning to hunt, a .22 shell—making its way, spinning nicely, held steady by its rotations—follows a clear trajectory to his chest through what, if it were slowed down enough, might be the most beautiful moment in Michigan history.

COVE

Just over the bridge, ten miles west of St. Ignace, overlooking the long southward cusp of Lake Michigan, a view stretching all the way down to Chicago, where on certain summer nights the sky mirage of that great city could be seen thrown against the clouds; just up from a row—six in all—of ramshackle summer shacks rented by the week, with their cracked clapboards and warped sandy floors; not far down Route 86, where, at the roadside trinket stand, built in the shape of a giant teepee, standing as testament to the falsity of history, supposedly native artifacts could be bought. There was a long-haired beauty up there working behind the counter for her father, a girl named Sky who had the most exquisite deep pooling eyes and deep brown skin, and who served the customers with a coy softness, a flirtatious energy that sold the goods and made for longing in the stiff sunburned legs of the tourists; up in the cove, below the dune head, below a line of pines that gave into the wind with a soft murmur—a dry windblown hiss that seemed rooted in eternity and, one has to presume, was the last thing s/he heard upon fading away: pine needles succumbing to the whims of the wind, the wind itself bringing in the smell of the lake, not a salty or sea smell but something else, a deeper murk, a place where in the winter the solitude fell down upon the edge of the lake with the towering, crusty collection of waves compiled into ice palaces, where only the sound of water and ice communed with the windblown trees itching the sky. Just over the bridge, to the west, not far from the same place where, years before, Marquette stood staring at the wide vista; just thirty-five miles north of the huge mansions hugging the shore of Little Traverse Bay, fed by Chicago tycoon wealth, with their trimmed manicured yards stretching down to private beachfront; just fifty miles from the small creek draining urgently into Walloon Lake, gurgling and bubbling over stones, the body was found in the cove by the state policeman Warren Graves, who was pretty sure that the case would not be solved because four seasons had passed over the corpse, taking away skin and flesh and evidence. The officer turned away, walked down the cove, crossed the highway to the beach, where he smoked a cigarette and stared with deliberate concentration off into the water, which caught the wind with flecks of waves not more than an inch high, which in turn collected the light of the setting sun in long corrugated sheets of orange-red. Even the most inattentive observer could not help but make the clear-cut connection between the two things: the result of the violence (natural or otherwise) up in the cove behind Warren Graves, and the blood-red aftermath of a day spreading over the water, in front.

THE SECRET GOLDFISH

He had a weird growth along his dorsal fin, and that gape-mouth grimace you see in older fish. Way too big for the tank, too, having outgrown the standard goldfish age limit. Which is, what? About one month? He was six years old—outlandishly old for a fish. One afternoon, Teddy, as he was called then, now just Ted, took sudden notice of the condition of Fish's tank; a wedge of sunlight plunged through the window of his bedroom and struck the water's surface, disappearing. The water was so clotted it had become a solid mass, a putty within which Fish was presumably swimming, or dead. Most likely dead. Where's Fish? Where's Fish? Teddy yelled to his mom. She came into his room, caught sight of the tank, and gave a small yelp. Once again, a fish had been neglected.

Everyone knows the story. The kids beg and plead: Please, please get us a fish (or a dog), we'll feed it, we will, honest, we'll take care of it and you won't have to do a single thing. We'll clean the tank walls with the brush and make sure the filter charcoal is replaced regularly and refill the water when it evaporates. Please, please, we can handle it, we're old enough now, we are, it'll be so much fun, it will, so much fun. But in the end they don't. They dump too much food in no matter how often they're told to be careful, to use just a pinch, and even after they've read Biblical-sounding fables about the fish who ate too much and grew too large for its bowl, shattering the sides, they watch gleefully while he consumes like mad, unable to stop. It's fun to watch him eat, to witness the physical manifestation of a fact: the level of Fish's hunger is permanently set to high. In the metaphysics of the fish universe, gluttony is not a sin. The delicate wafers of food fall lightly onto the water, linger on the surface tension, and are broken apart on infinitely eager lips. She overfeeds, too (on the days when she's pretty sure the kids haven't fed him). Her shaking mechanics are sloppy. The light flakes become moist, collude, collect their inertia, and all too often fall out of the can in a large clump. Really, she hasn't neglected the poor fish. "Neglect" seems a word too heavy with submerged intent. Something was bound to slip to the side amid the chaos of the domestic arena. But Fish has sustained himself in terrible conditions. He is the king of all goldfish survivors.

Her own childhood goldfish—named Fred—ended his days in Grayling Pond, a hole near her house in northern Michigan, dug out by the state D.N.R. on a pond-production grant. (Why the Great Lakes state needed more ponds is anyone's guess.) Garnished with a wide band of lily pads, the water a pale yellow, speckled with skeeter-bug ripples, the pond was close to becoming a marsh. Hope you survive, Fred, her father had said as he slopped the fish out of the pail and into the pond. She did not forget the sight of her beloved fish as he slipped from the lip of the bucket and rode the glassine tube of water into the pond. The rest of the summer she imagined his orange form—brilliantly bright and fluorescent against the glimmer of water—in a kind of slow-motion replay. Dumbest animals on earth, she remembered her father adding. Nothing dumber than a carp. Maybe a catfish, or your goddamn mother.

Not long after that afternoon at Grayling Pond, her father left the house in a fit of rage. Gone for good, her mother said. Thank Christ. Then, few months later he was killed in a freak accident, crushed between hunks of ice and the hull of a container ship in Duluth. Superior's slush ice was temperamental that winter, chewing up the coastline, damaging bulkheads. Her father had signed on as one of the men who went down with poles and gave furtive pokes and prods, in the tradition of those Michigan rivermen who had once dislodged logjams with their peaveys and pike poles, standing atop the timber in their spiked boots, playing with magnificent forces. Accounts varied, but the basic story was that the ice shifted, some kind of crevasse formed, and he slipped in. Then the lake gave a heave and his legs were crushed, clamped in the jaw of God's stupid justice. As she liked to imagine it, he had just enough time to piece together a little prayer asking for forgiveness for being a failure of a father ("Dear Heavenly Father, forgive me for my huge failings as a father to my dear daughter and even more for my gaping failure as a husband to my wife") and for dumping Fred ("and for getting rid of that fish my daughter loved more than me"), and then to watch as the pale winter sun slipped quickly away while the other men urged him to remain calm and told him that he'd be fine and they'd have him out in a minute or so, while knowing for certain that they wouldn't.

Long after her father was gone, she imagined Fred lurking in the lower reaches of Grayling Pond, in the coolest pockets, trying to conserve his energy. Sometimes, when she was cleaning upstairs and dusting Teddy's room, she would pause in the deep, warm, silent heart of a suburban afternoon and watch Fish as he dangled asleep, wide-eyed, unmoving, just fluffing his fins softly on occasion. One time she even tried it herself, standing still, suspended in the dense fluid of an unending array of demanding tasks—cleaning, cooking, washing, grocery shopping, snack-getting—while outside the birds chirped and the traffic hissed past on the parkway.

∴

The marriage had fallen apart abruptly. Her husband—who worked in the city as a corporate banker and left the house each morning at dawn with the *Times*, still wrapped in its bright-blue delivery bag, tucked beneath his arm—had betrayed his vows. One evening he'd arrived home from work with what seemed to be a new face: his teeth were abnormally white. He'd had them bleached in the city. (In retrospect, she saw that his bright teeth were the first hint of his infidelity.) He had found a dentist on Park Avenue. Soon he was coming home late on some nights and not at all on others under the vague pretense of work obligations. In Japan, he explained, people sleep overnight in town as a sign of their dedication to business; they rent cubicles just wide enough for a body, like coffins, he said, and for days when he did not return she thought of those small compartments and she chose to believe him. (Of course I know about the Japanese, she had said, emphatically.) Then one night she found him in the bathroom with a bar of soap, rubbing it gently against his wedding ring—It's too tight, he said. I'm just trying to loosen it. When others were perplexed by the fact that she had not deduced his infidelity, picked up on the clues, during those fall months, she felt compelled (though she never did) to describe the marriage in all of its long complexity—fifteen years—starting with the honeymoon in Spain: the parador in Chincón, outside Madrid, that had once been a monastery, standing naked with him at the balcony door in the dusky night air listening to the sounds of the village and the splash of the pool. She had given up her career for the relationship, for the family. She had given up plenty in order to stay home for Teddy and Annie's formative years, to make sure those brain synapses formed correctly, to be assured that the right connections were fused. (Because studies had made it clear that a kid's success depended on the first few years. It was important to develop the fine motor skills, to have the appropriate hand play, not to mention critical reasoning skills, before the age of four!) So, yes, she guessed the whole decision to give herself over to the domestic job had been an act of free will, but now it felt as though the act itself had been carried out in the conditions of betrayal that would eventually unfold before her.

∴

Fish had come into the family fold in a plastic Baggie of water, bulging dangerously, knotted at the top, with a mate, Sammy, who would end up a floater two days later. Pet Universe had given free goldfish to all the kids on a preschool field trip. In less than a year, Fish had grown too big for his starter bowl and begun to tighten his spiralled laps, restricted in his movements by his gathering bulk and the glass walls of the bowl. Then he graduated to a classic five-gallon bowl where, over the course of the next few years, he grew, until one afternoon, still deep in what seemed to be a stable domestic situation, with the kids off at school, she went out to Pet Universe and found a large tank and some water-prep drops and a filter unit, one that sat on the rim and produced a sleek, fountainlike curl of water, and some turquoise gravel, and a small figurine to keep the fish company: a cartoonish pirate galleon—a combination of Mark Twain riverboat and man-of-war—with an exaggerated bow and an orange plastic paddle wheel that spun around in the tank's currents until it gobbed up and stuck. The figurine, which was meant to please the eyes of children, had that confused mix of design that put commercial viability ahead of the truth. Teddy and Annie hated it. Ultimately, the figure did serve one purpose. It rearranged the conceptual space of the tank and gave the illusion that Fish now had something to do, something to work around, during his languorous afternoon laps, and she found herself going in to watch him, giving deep philosophical consideration to his actions: Did Fish remember that he had passed that way before? Was he aware of his eternal hell, caught in the tank's glass grip? Or did he feel wondrously free, swimming—for all he knew—in Lake Superior, an abundant, wide field of water, with some glass obstructions here and there? Was he basically free of wants, needs, and everything else? Did he wonder at the food miraculously appearing atop the surface tension, food to be approached with parted lips? One evening, after observing Fish, when she was at the sink looking out the window at the yard, she saw her husband there, along the south side, holding his phone to his ear and lifting his free hand up and down from his waist in a slight flapping gesture that she knew indicated that he was emotionally agitated.

Shortly after that, the tank began to murk up. Through the dim months of January and February, the filter clotted, the flow stopped and stringy green silk grew on the lip of the waterfall. The murk thickened. In the center of the darkness, Fish swam random patterns and became a sad, hopeless entity curled into his plight. He was no longer fooled by his short-term memory into thinking he was eternally free. Nor was he bored by the repetitive nature of his laps, going around the stupid ship figurine, sinking down into the gravel, picking—typical bottom-feeder—for scraps. Instead, he was lost in the eternal roar of an isotropic universe, flinging himself wildly within the expanding big bang of tank murk. On occasion, he found his way to the light and rubbed his eye against the glass, peering out in a judgmental way. But no one was there to see him. No one seemed available to witness these outward glances. Until the day when Teddy, now just Ted, noticed and said Mom, Mom, the tank, and she went and cleaned it, but only after she had knocked her knuckle a few times on the glass and seen that he was alive, consumed in the dark but moving and seemingly healthy. Then she felt awe at the fact that life was sustainable even under the most abhorrent con-ditions. She felt a fleeting—connection between this awe and the possibility that God exists. But then she reminded herself that it was only Fish. Just frickin' Fish, she thought. Here I am so weepy and sad, trying to make sense of my horrible situa-tion, that something like this will give me hope. Of course, she was probably also thinking back to that afternoon, watching her father sluice Fred down into the warm waters of the shal-low pond in Michigan. Her memory of it was profoundly clear. The vision of the fish itself—pristine and bright orange—travelling through the water as it spilled from the bucket was exact and perfect.

She set to work scooping out the water with an old Tupperware bowl, replacing it in increments so the chlorine would evaporate, driving to Pet Universe to get another cotton filter, some water-clarifying drops, and a pound sack of activated charcoal nuggets. She disassembled the pump mechanism—a small magnet attached to a ring of plastic that hovered, embraced by a larger magnet. Somehow the larger magnet cooperated with the magnet on the plastic device and used physical laws of some sort to suck the water up and through the filter, where it cascaded over the wide lip and twisted as it approached the surface. It seemed to her as her fingers cleaned the device that it was not only a thing of great simplicity and beauty, but also something much deeper, a tool meant to sustain Fish's life, and in turn, his place in the family. The afternoon was clear, blue-skied, wintry bright—and out the kitchen window she saw the uncut lawn, dark straw brown, matted down in van Gogh swirls, frosted with cold. Past the lawn, the woods, through which she could see the cars moving on the parkway, stood stark and brittle in the direct implications of the winter light. It was a fine scene, embarrassingly suburban, but certainly fine. Back upstairs, she saw Fish swimming jauntily in his new conditions and she was pretty sure that he was delighted, moving with swift strokes from one end of the tank to the other, skirting the figurine professionally, wagging his back fin—what was that called, was it the caudal fin?—

fashionably, like a cabaret dancer working her fan. A beautiful tail, unfurling in a windswept motion in the clearing water. When she leaned down for a closer look, it became apparent that the fin was much, much larger than it seemed when it was in action and twining in on itself. When Fish paused, it swayed open beautifully—a fine, healthy, wide carp tail. Along his sides, he had the usual scars of an abused fish, a wound or two, a missing scale, a new, smaller growth of some kind down near his anal fin. But otherwise he seemed big, brutally healthy, still blinking off the shock of the sudden glare.

∴

Then the tank fell back into its murk, got worse, stank up, and became, well, completely, utterly, fantastically murky. Here one might note tangentially: if, as Aristotle claims, poetry is something of graver import than history—partly because of the naturalness of its statements—then Fish was more important than any domestic history, because Fish was poetic, in that he had succumbed to the darkness that had formed around him, and yet he was unwilling to die or; rather, he *did not* die. He kept himself alive. He kept at it. Somehow he gathered enough oxygen from the water—perhaps by staying directly under the trickle that made its way over the lip of the filter. Of course, by nature he was a bottom-feeder, a mud fish, accustomed to slime and algae and to an environment that, for other fish, would be insufferable. No trout could sustain itself in these conditions. Not even close. A good brookie would've gone belly up long ago. A brookie would want cool pockets of a fast-moving stream, sweet riffles, bubbling swirls, to live a good life. But Fish stood in his cave of slime, graver than the history of the household into which his glass enclave had been placed: Dad packing his suitcases, folding and refolding his trousers and taking his ties off the electric tie rack and carefully folding them inside sheets of tissue, and then taking his shoes and putting each pair, highly glossed oxfords (he was one of the few to make regular use of the shoeshine stand at Grand Central), into cotton drawstring sacks, and then emptying his top dresser drawer, taking his cufflinks, his old wallets, and a few other items. All of this stuff, the history of the house, the legal papers signed and sealed and the attendant separation agreement and, of course, the divorce that left her the house—all this historical material was transpiring outside the gist of Fish. He could chart his course and touch each corner of the tank and still not know shit. But he understood something. That much was clear. The world is a mucky mess. It gets clotted up, submerged in its own gunk. End of story.

He brushed softly against the beard of algae that hung from the filter device, worked his way over to the figurine, leaned his flank against her side, and felt the shift of temperature as night fell—Teddy liked to sleep with the window cracked a bit—and the oxygen content increased slightly as the water cooled. During the day, the sun cranked through the window, the tank grew warm, and he didn't move at all, unless someone, came into the room and knocked on the tank or the floor, and then he jerked forward slightly before quickly settling down. A few times the downstairs door slammed hard enough to jolt him awake. Or there was a smashing sound from the kitchen. Or voices, "What in the world should we do?" "I would most certainly like this to be amicable, for the sake of the kids." Or a shoe striking the wall in the adjacent master bedroom. At times he felt a kinship with the figurine, as if another carp were there alongside him, waiting, hovering. Other times he felt a slight kinship with the sides of the tank, which touched his gill flaps on those occasions when he went in search of light. God, if only he knew that he, Fish, was at the very center of the domestic arena, holding court with his own desire to live. He might have died happily right there! But he was not a symbolic fish. He seemed to have no desire to stand as the tragic hero in this drama.

∴

Sent out, told to stay out, the kids were playing together down in the yard so that, inside, the two central figures, Dad and Mom, might have one final talk. The kids were standing by the playhouse—which itself was falling to decrepitude, dark-gray smears of mildew growing on its fake logs— pretending to be a mom and a dad themselves, although they were a bit too old and self-conscious for playacting. Perhaps they were old enough to know that they were faking it on two levels, regressing to a secondary level of playacting they'd pretty much rejected but playing Mom and Dad, anyway, Teddy saying, I'm gonna call my lawyer if you don't settle with me, and Annie responding, in her high, sweet voice, I knew you'd lawyer up on me, I just knew it, and then both kids giggling in that secretive, all-knowing way they have. Overhead, the trees were fuzzed with the first buds of spring, but it was still cold, and words hovered in vapor from their mouths and darkness was falling fast over the trees, and beyond the trees the commuter traffic hissed unnoticed.

If you were heading south on the Merritt Parkway, on the afternoon of April 3rd, and you happened to look to your right through the trees after Exit 35, you might've seen them, back beyond the old stone piles, the farm fences that no longer held significance except maybe as a reminder of the Robert Frost poem about good fences and good neighbors and all of that: two kids leaning against an old playhouse while the house behind them appeared cozy, warm, and clearly, expensive. A fleeting tableau without much meaning to the commuting folk aside from the formulaic economics of the matter: near the parkway = reduced value, but an expensive area + buffer of stone walls + old trees + trendiness of area = more value.

There is something romantic and heartening about seeing those homes through the trees from the vantage of the parkway—those safe, confided Connecticut lives. Inside the house, the secret goldfish is going about his deeply moving predicament, holding his life close to the gills, subdued by the dark but unwilling to relinquish his cellular activities, the Krebs cycle still spinning its carbohydrate breakdown. The secret goldfish draws close to the center of the cosmos. In the black hole of familial carelessness, he awaits the graceful moment when the mother, spurred on by Teddy, will give yet another soft shriek. She'll lean close to the glass and put her eye there to search for Fish. Fish will be there, of course, hiding in the core of the murk near the figurine, playing possum, so that she will, when she sees him, feel the pitiful sinking in her gut—remembering the preschool field trip to Pet Universe, and a sorrow so deep it will send her to her knees to weep. She'll think of the sad little pet funeral she had hoped to perform when Fish died (when Fish's sidekick died, Dad flushed him away): a small but deeply meaningful moment in the back yard, with the trowel, digging a shoebox-size hole, putting the fish in, performing a small rite ("Dear Lord, dear Heavenly Father, dear Fish God, God of Fish, in Fish's name we gather here to put our dear Fish to rest"), and then placing atop the burial mound a big rock painted with the word "Fish". It would be a moment designed to teach the children of the ways of loss, and the soft intricacies of seeing something that was once alive now dead, and to clarify that sharp defining difference, to smooth it over a bit, so that they will remember the moment and know, later, recalling it, that she was a good mother, the kind who would hold pet funerals.

But Fish is alive. His big old carp gills clutch and lick every tiny trace of oxygen from the froth of depravity in the inexplicably determinate manner that only animals have. He will have nothing to do with this household. And later that evening, once Dad is gone, they'll hold a small party to celebrate his resurrection, because they had assumed—as was natural in these circumstances—that he was dead, or near enough to death to be called dead, having near-death visions, as the dead are wont: that small pinpoint of light at the end of the tunnel and visions of an existence as a fish in some other ethery world, a better world for a fish, with fresh clear water bursting with oxygen and other carp large and small in communal bliss and just enough muck and mud for good pickings. After the celebration, before bedtime, they'll cover the top of the clean tank in plastic wrap and, working together, moving slowly with the unison of pallbearers, being careful not to slosh the water, carry it down the stairs to the family room, where with a soft patter of congratulatory applause they'll present Fish with a new home, right next to the television set.